T0070389

COMMANDER WALKER

ROBERT LLEWELLYN JONES

COMMANDER WALKER

Copyright © 2022 Robert Llewellyn Jones.

All rights reserved. No part of this book may be used or reproduced by any means,
graphic, electronic, or mechanical, including photocopying, recording, taping or by
any information storage retrieval system without the written permission of the author
except in the case of brief quotations embodied in critical articles and reviews.

This is a work of fiction. All of the characters, names, incidents, organizations, and dialogue
in this novel are either the products of the author's imagination or are used fictitiously.

iUniverse books may be ordered through booksellers or by contacting:

iUniverse
1663 Liberty Drive
Bloomington, IN 47403
www.iuniverse.com
844-349-9409

Because of the dynamic nature of the Internet, any web addresses or links contained in
this book may have changed since publication and may no longer be valid. The views
expressed in this work are solely those of the author and do not necessarily reflect the
views of the publisher, and the publisher hereby disclaims any responsibility for them.

Any people depicted in stock imagery provided by Getty Images are models,
and such images are being used for illustrative purposes only.
Certain stock imagery © Getty Images.

ISBN: 978-1-6632-4025-5 (sc)
ISBN: 978-1-6632-4026-2 (e)

Print information available on the last page.

iUniverse rev. date: 06/24/2022

In honor of Robin,
treasured husband, father, friend,
and lover of the sea.

"Where the ocean meets the sky, he'll be sailing."

ACKNOWLEDGMENTS

I'm not sure exactly who read/commented on chapters or drafts of this book. I know that Robin asked for feedback from several people. Thanks to all who encouraged him to finish it. Those who gave him confidence to press on include but are not limited to Gregory Frost, Daniel Merchant, Chris Hatch, Joe Schaller, Lanie Zera, Don Lafferty, Baille Cimino, and Neely Jones/Merchant.

Others who helped get this into print include the staff at Iuniverse, Cordelia Biddle, Dennis Delman, Nick Cimino, and Kimberly Leahy.

Although he didn't know his deadline was approaching, Robin worked intensely during his final weeks, determined to finish his first draft. If he'd had time to revise it into a second, no doubt he'd have made changes. At the very least, he'd have corrected commas, added a bit of this, deleted a chunk of that, expanded, condensed, edited, and altered, as is the common practice. (The first draft, in my experience, is usually kind of incomplete, rough and unpolished.)

But Robin's, as you'll see, is not a typical first draft. He gave much thought to his characters, their relationships, and actions. Their story is tight and compelling. In fact, Robin had plans to take several of them forward into two or three more novels, revealing secrets of their pasts (some of which are alluded to but unresolved in this book), creating conflicts, testing loyalties, and challenging courage in further nautical adventures.

Sadly, we'll never know to what ports Commander Albert Walker might have sailed (or with whom). We can only savor this first glimpse at a brave, adventurous, sea-loving naval officer, who, at his best and most heroic moments, bears some little resemblance to his creator.

I hope you enjoy COMMANDER WALKER, and that, as you sail off to future points, you'll carry the memory of its dear, sorely missed author in your heart.

Merry Jones

1

A man in a boat cloak pushed a barrow along a row of warehouses on the Thames at Woolwich. A steady rain rattled off a small tarpaulin that covered the barrow. The lantern the man carried did little to dispel the darkness. The man stopped and held the lantern up to see the number plate on one warehouse, then lowered it and moved on. Two warehouses farther down, he stopped again, looked at the number, put the lantern on the ground and undid the heavy latch on the warehouse door.

Iron wheels complained along an iron track as he heaved his weight against the door to slide it open just enough to pull the barrow inside. Retrieving the lantern, he closed the door and, leaving the barrow there, held the lantern ahead of him and walked about half of the length of the building. Naval stores were piled on each side. Rope, tar, oakum, blocks of various sizes, all suddenly left idle when the war with France had given way to an uneasy peace.

The man hung the lantern on a nail driven into one of the uprights that supported the roof. The weak light it gave off revealed an open hatch in the floor. Water lapped gently against the pilings below. A cage lay on its side next to the hatch. The cage was a little more than two feet square and just over six feet tall. It would fit through the hatch comfortably. Three sides were made of wood; one was closed with iron bars. Two planks were missing from one side of the cage and lay next to it. An iron eyebolt was fastened to one corner of the top of the cage.

The man walked back to the barrow and pushed it down next to the hatch. He took off his cloak, hung it over the handles of the barrow and pulled off the tarp to reveal a man in a naval uniform, an officer. He lay on his side, gagged, blindfolded, and bound hand and foot. The officer struggled, tried to speak. The man ignored him, reached into the barrow and retrieved a hammer and a dozen nails. He placed these by the cage. Earlier, he had rigged a block and tackle from a beam above the hatch. He attached the lower block to the eyebolt on the top of the cage and took the slack out of the ropes, securing the bitter end to a cleat on the upright that held the lantern.

The naval officer struggled anew as the man dragged him out of the barrow and dumped him into the cage where the two boards were missing. The man continued to ignore the officer's struggles and moans as he carefully laid the first board in place. With a practiced skill, he drove three nails into pre-drilled holes in each end of the board, secured the second board in the same way and began to haul the cage upright with the block and tackle. The blocks squealed in protest as the rope took a strain and the cage scraped across the floor to swing free over the open hatch. The naval officer struggled to stand up.

The man lowered the cage about a foot and secured the rope again so that he could reach in and release the officer's hands and feet before he began to lower him again. The naval officer had been tied up for some time. His hands and fingers were stiff, and he could barely feel them, so the cage was well below the floor of the pier before he could make his hands work well enough to remove the gag and blindfold.

"Avast! Whoever you are, in the name of King, stop! Are you mad? What have I done to you? Hoist me up! I command you. 'Vast lowering. Haul away!"

The man ignored this and everything else the naval officer said as he carefully gauged the height of the cage above the water. Finally satisfied, he secured the rope to the cleat, donned his boat cloak, collected his hammer and lantern, and wheeled the barrow out of the warehouse, leaving the naval officer's pleadings and threats behind him. The Thames and the rising tide would do the rest of his work for him.

1 1

The single epaulet on his left shoulder indicated that the young man walking purposefully along the Strand was a commander in the Royal Navy, newly promoted from lieutenant. He was tall for the times, a little over six feet. His uniform hat, in the relatively new fore and aft style, covered a mass of unruly dark brown hair that he wore tied at the nape of his neck with a dark blue ribbon. He wore an expensively tailored uniform and the silver buckles on his shoes were clearly sterling, not pinchbeck.

As he turned onto Whitehall and closed on the Admiralty building, he reread the summons one last time, "Admiral Sir William Burns presents his compliments to Commander Albert Walker and requests, if it is convenient, that the Commander attend the Admiral at his chambers in Whitehall at ten of the clock the day following this."

It was, of course, always convenient for commanders to attend admirals. Walker had no idea what the admiral could want. He was far too junior to be given a command in this time of peace, and, from what Walker knew of the Admiralty, Burns did not have any great influence in its day-to-day operations.

A porter approached him as he entered the Admiralty building.

"Good morning, Commander Walker, this way please."

Walker had never been a frequent visitor to the Naval offices at Whitehall, so it was significant that the porter knew who he was and had obviously been waiting for him to arrive. He followed the porter up a flight of stairs and down a long hallway on the second floor. They passed the chambers of the great and powerful and turned down a narrow corridor

3

that Walker had not noticed as they approached it. They walked back some thirty feet into increasing darkness until the porter stopped and opened a small door on his right.

"In here, Commander, if you will."

The door led into an office where several clerks worked at high-topped desks. Shelves containing files of paper and journals lined the walls. Walker was careful to tip the porter as he took his leave, closing the outer door behind him.

One of the clerks nodded to Walker, opened the door to an inner office. "Commander Walker is here," he said, and, with a slight bow, motioned him in.

Admiral Burns was a short, stout, balding man with a round, ruddy, friendly face. He stood with his back to a small fire with a sheaf of papers in his hand. His waistcoat was only partially buttoned, and his neck cloth was a bit askew. His uniform coat, well-worn and slightly out of style, hung on a hook on the wall. The walls of the room were, like the outer office, lined with shelves of files and journals.

When Walker entered the chamber, Burns put the papers down on top of a cluttered desk and greeted him with a firm handshake and a warm smile. "Ah, Commander Walker, it's good of you to come on such short notice. Sit down please."

Walker bowed slightly. "It is my pleasure, sir."

"Have a seat, have a seat," the admiral said, pointing to a chair in front of his desk. Walker sat down, and the admiral took his seat behind it.

"Congratulations on your promotion, by the way. It was well deserved, and too long in coming if you ask me. I read about your part in the taking of that French corvette. Damn shame about this peace, or you'd have a command by now. Your father's quite pleased, you know."

Walker did not know. His wealthy father had not been pleased when he had chosen a career in the navy, and the subject rarely came up between them. What Burns said, though, told Walker two things. First, that Burns was well-connected. Walker's father was a member of Parliament who had held cabinet portfolios over the years. If Burns was privy to his father's thoughts on family matters, then he moved in a lofty circle, indeed. Second, that Burns had taken the time to follow, or at least to research Walker's career. He'd led a small boat assault at night on a French ship moored under a well-manned fort. It was that action that had led to his promotion, and the admiral was right: He would have a command now if the war had gone on.

"Something to drink, Commander?" Without waiting for an answer, the admiral leaned to his right called to the outer office, "Forbes, two glasses of claret, won't you?"

Walker was not much of a drinker; one glass never seemed to be enough. He never drank hard spirits and wine only with meals, but this was no time to refuse.

Burns turned back to Walker.

"So tell me a bit about the taking of that corvette. It's one thing to read about these things in the *Gazette,* but it's always better to hear it first at hand."

The admiral was obviously not going to be rushed into revealing the reason for Walker's visit. Forbes brought in the two glasses of wine. They each took a sip, and Walker began.

"Well, sir, we chased her until she ran in and anchored under the guns of a small fort. We beat about out of range of the fort for some hours, hoping that the wind would shift and the Frenchman would come out and fight. The wind, however, stayed stubbornly onshore. There would be no moon that night, so Captain Martin decided to take advantage of the dark and send in a small force in boats cut her out. I volunteered to lead the party."

"Of course," said the admiral, nodding his head as if it were the most common thing in the world to want to lead a group of sailors and marines in fragile wooden boats, armed only with cutlasses and pistols, against a ship armed with eighteen-pounder cannon protected by a shore battery of what were probably thirty-two pounders.

"While there was still plenty of light, Captain Martin sailed away from the island, as if we had given up on the corvette. We launched the boats as soon as we were hull down to the fort and started to row back as the sun began to set.

"The moon was just new and there were some clouds. We could see the Frenchie well enough against the shore, but we hoped we'd blend into the sea and she wouldn't discover us until it was too late to mount a good defense. In that, we were fortunate. I was in the launch. Lieutenant Samuel

Mink commanded the cutter. We approached slowly under muffled oars. My boat was about ten boat-lengths away before the watch aboard the corvette raised the alarm. Lieutenant Mink was closer still. I had taken the precaution to double-bank the oars in both boats, so we were able to close with the ship quickly after they saw us, and board and engage the ship's crew before they could get at all organized. In that regard, I cannot commend Lieutenant Mink's actions enough. The smoke from his assault forward had already drifted aft by the time my party and I had gained the afterdeck."

At the mention of drifting gun smoke, the admiral shifted in his chair. In his younger years he had known the acrid bite of that smoke all too well, and at Walker's mention of it, his nostrils flared to it once again. He sniffed audibly and leaned forward as Walker continued.

"Lieutenant Mink led his men over the bows, overwhelmed the men coming up out of the forward hatches, and secured those hatches quickly. Without that, I don't know that we would have accomplished the task with such a short butcher's bill. There were none killed in our crew and only a few minor wounds. The officers and men aft surrendered to me quickly when they realized that Mink and his men controlled the foredeck. By then the onshore wind had died and a light breeze was beginning to blow off the land. Under main and topsails, we were able to make slow but steady progress seaward."

"And the fort gave you no trouble?"

The admiral could imagine the tension onboard the corvette as she clawed off the land, everyone on board, even the prisoners, praying that the fort would hold fire and the wind hold fair.

"They fired a few rounds, but I believe it was out of frustration more than an attempt to do any damage. Every shot was well wide of us. The only way to stop us after we gained the corvette was to destroy it and its crew, and they just weren't about that."

"It's good of you to mention Lieutenant Mink in that way. The *Gazette* gave him credit only as your second, with no details. Excellent work on both your parts, a job well done."

Burns sat erect and pulled his chair into the desk. Leaning forward, he said, "But we both know I didn't ask you here just to talk shop, so let's get on with it, shall we?"

Walker nodded and took another sip of wine.

"Do you recall the incident of the *Diligence*?" the admiral began.

"She was a sixth-rate, lost just before the peace, was she not?"

"Exactly," Burns said, tapping his desk with a finger. "According to the record of the court-martial, she was attacked by a much larger French ship on her way home from the West Indies. Her captain did the prudent thing and tried to get away. The *Diligence*'s nine-pounders against the Frenchman's heavier guns, and a two to one advantage in guns, she was no match. It would have been suicide to take her on."

Walker nodded in agreement. There was no shame in a captain of an overmatched vessel trying to save his men and his ship.

"So, her captain, Jenkins, James Jenkins it was, turned away, set all sail. He was making good his escape, too, until the Frenchie's bow chaser got in a lucky shot at her mizzen rigging, cut it by the rail, and set the mizzen mast crashing forward into the main rigging, leaving her unmanageable.

"Before the Frenchman could close her, though, a gale that had been building up blew through. The wind set against the Frenchie and caught the *Diligence* broadside on. Knocked her down almost on her beam ends." Burns swept a forearm down as he said this, mimicking the fatal roll of the ship.

Walker shifted in his chair. He had weathered many storms and seen spars carried away, but he could only imagine the chaos on board the *Diligence* as she lay on her side in a tangle of spars and rigging.

"Jenkins had been lightening her to speed her up. Most of her guns and heavy stores had gone overboard, so she didn't sink straight away. Jenkins had the crew cut the windward rigging, hoping to right her. That did bring the little ship up a bit, but it caused the mainmast to snap. By now she'd taken on a lot of water, and Jenkins feared she wouldn't swim for long. So he had the survivors - there were damn few by this time, according to the record - load what stores they could into the launch and the cutter, and off they set. Jenkins actually made it to Jamaica, but the cutter got separated from him during one night and was never seen again, so damn few of them survived it altogether. Still, a nice trick of seamanship."

"Nice indeed," Walker agreed, nodding. "But what of the Frenchman?"

"The Frenchie lost some rigging, too, but must have been too busy saving herself to give any more thought to the chase just then. According to the testimony, she was last seen drifting off to leeward."

"How many actually made it to Jamaica?"

"Six, as I recall. They court-martialed Jenkins, of course, but the court exonerated him. He came off pretty much the hero of the affair. If we'd still been at war, he'd have been given a new ship straightaway, but the best they could do for him was a position at the dockyard in Woolwich. Not command, but better than half-pay, surely."

The admiral stood and began to pace in front of the fire. Walker turned in his chair.

"Now, here's where this gets interesting: Jenkins disappeared some days ago, never showed up at the dockyard one morning. A search initially turned up nothing, but he was found the next day, quite by accident, near death and apparently quite mad."

"Mad, sir?"

"Raving mad, and given his circumstances when found, I can't blame him. He was found in a cage suspended in the Thames from inside a storehouse pier."

"A cage, sir?" Walker interjected. The admiral sat again and reached for his glass.

"Yes, about two by two by six or so, wood on three sides and iron bars on the fourth, appeared to have been made just for the occasion. It's still at the pier where he was found. He could have been there a full day, since the night he disappeared, but I suspect it was not that long. I doubt he could have survived more than a tide, if that. Two clerks who went in to take inventory noticed lines running down through a hatch in the floor and found the cage suspended from them. Water was up near its top, just enough room for him to breathe, and the tide was about to crest. They got him out just in time."

"I saw nothing of this in the papers, sir."

Burns got up and again paced before the fire. "No, we've kept it quiet. In part for Captain Jenkins' sake, and of course, the less talk in the *Times* about raving lunatics walking about in naval uniforms, the better. So this is all on the hush hush, for now, until we see if Jenkins will come to his senses, and until we know more about what happened to him. That's where you fit in, Walker."

Walker cocked his head. "Me, sir? In what way?"

"If you'll take it on, I'd like you to try to find out what happened to Jenkins, and what it may have to do with the loss of his ship. You'll have the full record of the court-martial, access to Jenkins and the survivors of the *Diligence,* and, of course, my full support. What do you say?"

Walker certainly had the time, and one rarely said no to an admiral, but even more, he was intrigued, particularly by the fact that the admiral thought that Jenkins' disappearance was somehow linked with the loss of his ship.

"Yes. Of course, I'll take it on. But what is the significance of the records of the court-martial?"

"If Jenkins had never disappeared and been found as he was, they would still be filed away somewhere and, eventually, forgotten. But, as I followed his trial and read the testimony, something kept nagging at me. Nothing I could put a finger on, mind you. Nothing, surely, that would warrant any official revisiting of the case. But something. So, when they found Jenkins as they did, I knew we had to do more than just find the man who kidnapped him. We have to know why, we have to know if there's more to this affair, and that's why I've asked you here."

"What was it in the record that roused your suspicions, sir?"

The admiral paused momentarily, considering the question, then sat back at his desk and said, "I'd rather not tell you. I'd rather you go into it with an open mind, have a fresh look and see what you find. I'll have the records of the court-martial sent to your home, along with the whereabouts of all the players, if you will, as best we know them, and the location of the pier where Jenkins was found. If you need my assistance, just ask. Oh, and I'll leave it to your discretion if you wish to engage anyone to work with you in this. Well, then, that's settled. Do you have any more questions of me?" the admiral asked, signaling that the interview was over.

Walker had many questions, beginning with why he had been chosen for this, but they could wait for another day.

"No, sir. I'm sure I shall, but not for now."

The admiral smiled and raised his glass. "To your success, then, Commander."

"Success, yes sir, thank you," Walker replied, and he raised his glass in return.

They drank, toasted the King, and the admiral called to the outer chamber, "James."

Walker rose and the two men shook hands. A clerk appeared in the doorway.

"Thank you again for coming on such short notice, commander. James, will you show Commander Walker the way out?"

"That's quite all right, sir. I can find my way."

"Not the way James will show you." The admiral smiled and nodded toward James to proceed. James led Walker out into the small hallway but turned to the right, away from the main hall, through a door and down a tight spiral stair that led to a door that opened into a recess in the back of the building.

"If you go out and turn to your right, and right again, you'll find yourself on the Strand, sir. And the admiral would be pleased if you'd use this entrance when you visit. Two quick knocks on the door upstairs, a pause and another knock will admit you."

"Thank you, James." Walker placed his hat on his head, stepped out into the sunshine and found himself on a gravel path. As he walked toward the Strand, he stopped and looked back to be sure he could find the recess again. It was between two large shrubs and, unless one looked for it, was not easy to see. Walker continued, turned right and walked on home.

| | |

The door to the Walker family's imposing townhouse opened for him as he approached it. The family's chief butler, Jessup, held the door for him as he held out his hand for Walker's hat. Jessup was above medium height, slim and erect. He wore his unruly graying brown hair tied at the nape of his neck in a dark blue ribbon. Jessup had worked for the Walker family in one position or another since before Walker was born, and had risen over the years to his lofty post. He rarely spoke but always seemed to appear when needed, often before one knew he would be needed. No one knew what he had done before coming to the family, but there was an old rumor among the servants that he'd once been a highwayman or something along that line.

As Jessup took Walker's hat, he said, "You have a letter, sir." He presented an envelope.

Walker immediately recognized the handwriting of his sister, Isadora. Breaking the seal, he scanned the message, which announced her imminent return from her latest visit to the country. He appreciated the advance notice; Isadora inevitably brought with her a flurry of social activity and a general upending of his usual solitary, well-structured life.

Jessup waited for Walker to slip the letter into his pocket before he continued. "Also, you have a visiter, a lieutenant Mink. He awaits your arrival in the drawing room."

"Mink, is it? Thank you, Jessup." Walker brightened and walked briskly toward the drawing room.

Lieutenant Samuel Mink and Walker had served together for some four years and had become close friends, with great respect for each other's abilities as seamen. Mink was a large man, not quite as tall as Walker but with a larger frame and a burst of dark wavy hair he parted down the middle that framed a bright open, Irish face. His ready smile endeared him to most everyone he met, especially the ladies. He was filling a heavy sliver flask with Walker's best brandy as Walker entered the drawing room.

"So you found the brandy straightaway, eh?"

Mink turned and laughed, "Well, I knew it would get damned lonely if it depended on you for company, so I thought it only proper to pay my respects to it." He slipped the flask into a pocket inside his waistcoat and embraced Walker.

"It's good to see you, Samuel, but I thought you were in Ireland."

"I was staying with a distant cousin on my mother's side, but his daughter somehow came upon the absurd notion that I was courting her, and when he asked my intentions, I thought it might be best to see how things were getting on with you in London."

"Walked a fine line with her, did you?"

"She is a wonderfully attractive young woman, and I may have overstepped, but matrimony was never in it."

"Never, of course." Walker grinned. "A narrow escape, then?"

"It was. Not that you are one to pass judgment, given your own unfortunate history."

"Now, Samuel, that was an entirely different circumstance. And it was not one from which I was attempting to escape."

"Nonetheless, Albert, escape you did."

"I hardly considered it an escape – I was eager to marry Anna."

"Nonetheless, it's been a few years now, has it not? You've become all but a recluse since that terribly unfortunate business. Tragic."

"I prefer not to discuss this subject."

"As do I. But it is all the more cause for you to join me at the upcoming Troubador Ball. Many of society's finest young ladies will be in attendance. It's time you rejoined the living. What say you?"

Walker knew of no such ball and generally avoided such frivolous occasions, but Mink pressed on. Presenting his copy of the invitation, he continued, "I am, as you know, well acquainted with the host and hostess, and they have repeatedly expressed their desire that I attend. Will you join me, then?"

Walker glanced at the invitation long enough to read that the gala was planned for the following Saturday. By then, given his new assignment, he hoped he would be launching, or possibly at sea.

"I'll consider it," he said. "While I do, though, please delay your own response to the hosts."

Mink looked puzzled, but replaced the invitation in his pocket.

Hoping to put an end to the matter, Walker put a hand on his friend's shoulder. "You'll stay with me while you're here." It was a statement, not a question. "I'll have Jessup set up your room."

Just as Walker turned to pull the bell rope to summon him, Jessup appeared in the doorway. "I've placed the lieutenant's things in the front room at the end of the upstairs hall, sir, and dinner is served."

"Come along to the dining room then, Samuel, I have a surprise for you there."

And indeed, he did. As they entered the room, Mink stopped in open astonishment.

"Darling? Cannon?" he exclaimed.

Two servants stood by the sideboard and greeted Mink with naval salutes and cheerful grins. Dressed in duck trousers and striped shirts, with their hair done down the back of their necks in neat braids, they were unmistakably seaman in the English Navy. William Darling was a boatswain's mate, Frederick Cannon was, improbably, a gunner's mate. They had served with Walker and Mink until their ship had paid off. Darling had straight black hair, an oval face and an olive complexion. Cannon's round face and impish grin was framed in light brown curls that somehow always avoided being braided. Both were capable, resourceful men that could be counted on no matter the circumstance.

"I brought them along with me because they were at loose ends, and I knew that mother and father would take the better part of the servants to the country house with them. Besides, I doubt this peace will last, and I may find myself in need of a good boatswain and a good gunner, and I can't think of two better."

"Nor I, Albert, nor I," Mink agreed, looking genuinely pleased. "It's good to see the both of you again."

"And good to see you too, sir," Cannon said. "Good to serve with you again."

Walker and Mink sat at one end of the long table in the house's formal dining room. As Darling presented a platter of sliced beef to Mink, Mink asked, "Tell me, men, how are you getting on, working in the house? Don't you miss the ship?"

Darling replied, "I miss the old barky, but there's much to be said for fresh meat and a warm, dry bed, sir."

As Cannon offered Walker a tray of boiled potatoes, he added, "Fresh meat and warm and dry is all right by me, but, tell the truth, I miss me hammock, sir, I do."

"Ah, hammocks," Mink said. "I missed mine, too, when I first put on a frock coat."

"You was in a hammock, Mr. Mink?" Darling stopped and stood upright, his eyes widening. "You was a seaman, came in through the hawse hole did ye?" he asked.

Walker laughed, "Go on, Samuel. Tell them how you turned what was to be a flogging into that first frock coat."

Mink was always ready to tell a story. He put down his knife and fork, turned toward Darling and Cannon, leaned back in his chair and began.

"Well, it was a good many years ago. I was an able seaman on the old *Dauntless*. Captain Peebles had her then. I liked to fill my idle hours with reading and took to 'borrowing' books from the sailing master, Andrews was his name, as I recall. I took them at first just because they were books, and I needed something to read, anything. But it turned out it was fascinating stuff, ship handling and navigation, and I took a particular liking to the celestial. I'd always been good with numbers, and there were numbers aplenty to play with there. But I got caught one day. Third lieutenant found me in the sailing master's things, taking a book back, and hauled me to the captain as a common thief. Wanted me given a couple dozen lashes for it.

"Lucky for me, old Peebles wasn't a flogging man and wanted first to hear what I had to say for myself. So I laid it on with him a bit heavy about my love for the service and wanting to better myself, and such. And that's where I sealed my fate. Old Peebles took me at my word. He called for

Andrews and told him he and the schoolmaster were to question me, find out if I was telling the truth, if I'd learned anything in all my reading."

Walker continued to eat as Mink warmed to his subject, and Darling and Cannon hung on each word.

"Well, Andrews and the schoolmaster, I forget his name, they quizzed me pretty good for an hour and more, everything from my ABCs to getting the barky underway to maneuvering, where was this star and that one, and what was one to do with them, boxing the compass, points of the wind. For the most part, I gave them as good as I got. All I wanted to do was to avoid the cat, slip back to my mess, and hope they all forgot about me as quick as they could. So, finally, Andrews takes me back to Peebles, and old Peebles asks him how I did. Imagine my surprise when the Master tells him I know as much or more than most of the young gentlemen, the midshipmen he's been trying to teach all this to. Peebles looks me in the eye a second or two, pulls at his ear, as he was known to do when he was thinking, and ups and says, 'Very well then, I'll rate him midshipman, here and now.'

"You can imagine my surprise when he turns to his clerk and says to him, 'Wiggins, make it so.'" Wiggins begins to scratch his pen in one of his journals.

"'Sir?' says I. 'Midshipman, sir?'

"'Midshipman,' he repeats, and says to the master, 'Take him along now, and get him settled in with the other young gentlemen.'

"Then he turns back to the papers on his desk. The interview is over, and I'm on my way to the midshipmen's berth."

Mink spread his arms and, with a big Irish grin and a sitting bow to his audience, said, "And that's how I turned a flogging into a frock coat."

After a round of applause and laughter, Walker asked, "Well, men, what about you? Shall I make you midshipmen one day if I have the chance?"

Darling spoke first, "Sir? Oh, no sir, please sir. The King's warrant's what I'd have, if I could, sir."

"Aye, sir," Cannon agreed. "No midshipman's berth for me. A warrant as gunner is what I'd want."

Darling and Cannon were no fools. If they could secure Navy Board warrants, they'd be at the very top of their professions. Unlike commissioned and petty officers, they could be assigned to a ship permanently, even if she were laid up and out of commission. The pay was good, and they had a clearly defined role in the operation of the ship. And they had surely seen too many midshipmen grow old in that rank, unable to pass the exam for lieutenant or lacking patronage, or both.

The conversation was cut short when Jessup walked in and announced to Walker, "Sir, an Admiralty messenger is here with a package. He insists that you sign for it personally."

"Of course," Walker said, turning to the door. "Show him in."

Darling and Cannon refilled the wine glasses and retreated to the back of the house as Mink applied himself to his roast beef and Jessup showed the courier into the room.

"Commander Walker?" the courier asked.

"I am," Walker replied.

"This is for you, sir," he said. He held out a large dispatch case in one hand and a receipt to be signed in the other.

"You may give the case to my man," Walker said, nodding to Jessup as he took a pencil from the courier and signed the receipt. Handing it back to the courier, he looked to Jessup who nodded his understanding that the courier would be compensated for his efforts. The courier and Jessup left the room.

"Admiralty courier, eh?" Mink said. "What have you been up to?"

"This is a project I was just asked to undertake, and it involves you, too."

Mink feigned a frightened surprise. "Me? Good Heavens, what have I done now? Have I been found out on something?"

Walker grinned. "No, Samuel, this involves you because I'd like you to join me in the endeavor."

"Well, that's different, then. What is it about?" Mink took a swallow of claret and sat back in his chair, ready to listen.

"Do you recall the affair of the *Diligence*? Happened some time before the peace. A captain Jenkins lost her in a storm while he was trying to outrun a superior French ship."

"James Jenkins, was it?"

"Yes, why?"

Mink waved his hand dismissively, "Bad sort, that one, from what I heard from someone who served under him. Flogs left and right, has his favorites among the officers and men, toadies that curry favor with him and lord it over the others."

"Hmmm, that could help explain why he was found in a cage hung under a dockyard's storage wharf."

Mink sat up. "A cage? Under a wharf?"

"That's what I was told. And when they hauled him up, he was quite mad. The Admiralty's asked me to look into it, see what's behind it all and if there's more to the loss of the *Diligence* than what the court martial found. It involves you because I'd like you to help me with it. What do you say?"

"Of course, and with pleasure. But what is the connection between the loss of his ship and the attack upon him?"

"I don't know. Admiral Burns says he found something about the court martial record that aroused his suspicion and he wanted me to read through and see what I found."

"Ah, so the dispatch case is the record. And who is this Burns?" Mink asked as he addressed the last of his roast beef.

"Admiral Sir William Burns. I'm not sure what his position is, but he works mostly on the hush-hush from what I've been able to gather."

"I've surely never heard of him," Mink replied. "But that doesn't signify much, given what little I know of Whitehall." He placed his napkin by his plate and said, "Well, shall we get on with it?" Mink rose and headed for the drawing room.

"Absolutely." Walker replied. As he stood to follow Mink, he called out, "Darling, coffee in the drawing room, if you will."

"Aye, Sir," came the reply from the butler's pantry as the two men crossed the hall.

The dispatch case was on a table just by the door. Jessup stood protectively next to it.

"Thank you, Jessup. That will be all for now. Oh, and tell Mrs. Anson that the lieutenant and I will have supper at my club tonight."

"Yes, sir." Jessup said, nodded to Mink, and left the room.

Mink watched as Walker broke the wax seal on the red ribbon that circled the case, opened it, and pulled out several bundles of paper, each bound in red ribbon. A letter addressed to Walker had been slipped under the ribbon on the first bundle. Walker broke the seal, unfolded the letter and scanned it quickly.

Turning to Mink, he said, "This tells us where Jenkins was found, where he is now and the names and last known addresses of the other survivors."

He handed it to Mink as Darling walked in with the coffee.

"Ah, yes, the coffee. Put it there on the sideboard, won't you? And stand by, I want you to deliver a letter. Samuel, what say you we pay a visit to Captain Jenkins? Does tomorrow at ten suit you?"

"Admirably."

Walker went to a writing desk at the far end of the room and scratched out a brief note, folded and sealed the paper.

"Samuel, read me the address of the hospital where they're keeping Jenkins."

He wrote the address on the note and handed it to Darling.

"Here you are. To this address with you, take Cannon along if you like, and tell whoever answers that you are instructed to await a reply."

"Very good, sir." Darling knuckled his brow in salute and turned to leave.

"'Vast there, Darling." Mink said as he fished two silver coins from a waistcoat pocket and tossed them to him. "That's a fair way to go. You'll want some refreshment on the way back."

Darling caught the coins and looked at Walker.

"Go on with you," Walker said. "But mind that that's for the way back."

As Darling disappeared down the hall, he said to Mink, "You'll spoil them, Samuel."

"You can't spoil good men, and those two are good men. Besides, you've probably overworked them. They deserve an hour in a good tavern."

"Overworked? There's precious little to do in the house in the first place without my parents and sister here, and turning two lusty young men loose in the servants' quarters isn't my idea of harsh duty."

"Nor mine. Perhaps I should look into that, see that they're behaving?" Mink said with a sly grin.

"You'll do nothing of the sort," Walker grinned back. "Mrs. Anson has her hands full already. The last thing she needs is an Irish rogue like you hanging about, no matter how charming he may be."

Mink laughed, poured himself a cup of coffee and added a bit of brandy to it while Walker went back to the papers on the table.

"Now then, to business."

Mink set his coffee down on a small table next to one of the two large wingback chairs facing the fireplace and joined Walker as he sorted the papers.

"Here we have the charges, findings, and disposition of the court, then the testimony of Jenkins and each of the survivors. Why don't you start with the charges and such, and I'll start on Jenkins' testimony? We'll each go through it all and see if we can turn up what Burns found."

Mink took the bundle Walker offered and sat down next to his coffee. Walker poured himself coffee, without brandy, and settled into the other wingback chair. The dying embers of a fire set to chase the morning chill glowed at their feet. They read, turned pages, read some more, exchanged papers, and read on through the afternoon.

I V

They were still reading when Cannon, visibly sober, entered the room.

"Beg pardon, sir, but 'ere's your answer from the doctor."

Walker took the note from Cannon and unfolded it. Mink stood and stretched as Walker read the reply written in the margin of his note.

"'Dr. Pearce presents his complements and will be pleased to receive Commander Walker at ten o'clock on the morrow.' So, there's our morning's work, Samuel, a visit to Dr. Pearce's Hospital and Asylum to see the doctor and Captain Jenkins. Cannon, if you and Darling could have the carriage ready at half nine tomorrow, that should suit."

"Aye sir, half nine it is," Cannon said. "And what time will you be wanting to leave for your club, sir?"

"What say you, Samuel? Is another hour at this enough for you?"

"Enough and more," he replied as he carried a stack of papers to the table.

"An hour, then, Cannon."

Cannon knuckled his brow and left the room.

Walker put the papers he had been reading on the table and poured himself the few drops that remained of the now cold coffee. "You first, Samuel. Tell me what you found."

Mink paused for a moment, staring out one of the tall windows that faced the street. He turned to Walker.

"I think it's a pack of lies. Whatever happened that day, it is not what was said in that court martial."

"Go on."

"Just look at what they said, each and every one told the same story in almost the same words. No matter where they were on that ship or what their assigned duty, every one saw the very same thing happen at the very same time. Think of it. Is a man in the waist going to see what a man on the poop sees, or the fellow at the masthead? And how does a man who was below know anything of what transpires topside? I tell you, Albert, old Burns was right. But it doesn't take a genius to see it. How did the court let all this flow past them without backing water?"

"I agree with you. In hindsight, particularly with what happened to Jenkins, it's obvious that the testimony was rehearsed. But remember that this was a very routine court martial. A captain had lost his ship and had to explain himself. Being damaged by a superior force, then losing your ship to a sudden gale is enough to exculpate anyone. Then too, Jenkins had a clear, if not spectacular naval record, and he'd gotten his little band of survivors to safety. His account was plausible and supported by the only witnesses. I don't know that I'd have pursued it had I sat on that court. But the admiral's right; the attempt on Jenkins puts it all in a different light."

"Only if we assume that the attempt is linked to the loss of the ship," Mink said. "If what I've heard of Jenkins is correct, it could just be someone settling an old score. And what, I wonder, was a somewhat senior captain doing commanding a sixth-rate?" Sixth-rates were the smallest of warships. Commanders were usually placed in charge of them.

"Points well taken, Samuel. So we have our work cut out for us. Let us see where tomorrow's visit leads," Walker said. He finished sorting the papers and returned them to the dispatch case, leaving Burns' letter on the standing desk. "But enough of this for today. It's time to freshen up. The carriage will be around shortly."

At that, Jessup appeared in the doorway.

"I've laid out fresh shirts and neck cloths for each of you and there's hot water for shaving. I've also had your best uniform coats overhauled. You'll find them laid out in your rooms, as well. Will there be anything else?"

"No, Jessup. Thank you," Walker said.

Jessup turned and left.

As they went up the stairs, Mink asked. "Does he anticipate everything? How do you suppose he does it? Where did he come from?"

"That's all a mystery to me. I grew up with him in the house and, as for where he came from, no one's quite sure. As I heard it, he found us, appeared at the country house one day, a young man looking for work. They set him to mucking out the stables, and he worked his way up from there."

"Nothing about where he came from, eh?"

They passed at the top of the stairs.

"Nothing. Father says he tried to get it out of him a few times, but all he'd say is that he came from a poor upbringing and had a hard life 'til he came to us, how grateful he was to father for all he'd done for him, and such. He always turned the subject around. And here's a curious thing: he was quite literate when he came to us. Despite his 'poor upbringing', he could read and write quite well, knew his numbers up and down. His skills made him all the more valuable as a servant, of course, but only deepened the mystery."

"Hmm, curious case, Albert. Certainly more there than meets the eye, eh? Ah, well, that's my room, I presume?" He pointed to an open doorway in the front of the hall.

"Indeed, it is. I'll meet you down the stairs."

V

The family's landau was waiting for them in front of the house. Walker and Mink got in. Cannon folded up the steps, closed the door, got up on the box and, with a shake of the reins, they were off. Darling drove. He and Cannon were dressed in white canvas trousers, short black jackets and flat black tarred hats. They had politely but firmly refused Walker's suggestion that they wear the livery of the Walker family footmen, which even Walker thought a bit foppish. And they were, after all, sailors.

As they rolled away into the street, Mink to Walker. "Tell me, Albert, what do you make of the sensation of seeing or being part of something you've experienced before."

"I've never given it much thought. I imagine it's finding oneself in a situation similar to one one's already experienced. How's that?"

"I don't know but what it goes beyond that," Mink replied, "Suppose we get a chance to live our lives over, a chance to do it right or make other choices. That sensation could be us catching a glimpse of the past life, and it might explain fellows like Jessup. Maybe he's been around a few times, knows the ropes so to speak. Not that he's lived a lot of lives as your butler, but just that he's been around enough times that he knows what's wanted of a man in a given situation."

"Multiple lives, eh? Have you been reading up on oriental beliefs?"

"No, no," Mink said, shifting in his seat and waving off the thought with one hand. "But think about this. You wanted to be a naval officer from your youngest days. Yet you come from a landed family who has never sent a son to sea, and your father was dead set against it. But here you are, a commander with a great career ahead of you. You handle a ship with the best of them. Could you not have lived before in preparation for this?"

Walker cocked his head to one side in thought for a second. "Come to think of it, I did have an early bent toward the sea." Walker turned toward Mink. "See how this fits into your theory. One day when I was a boy, about eight or so, I was in the carriage with my stepmother. We were stopped while they drove some cattle over across a street. As we sat there, I spotted an old cutlass in a curiosity shop window. For some reason I suddenly had to have that cutlass. I begged and pleaded with mother until she relented and sent a footman in to purchase it."

"So, does that explains the cutlass hung above the fireplace in the drawing room? Looking so wonderfully out of place under the family coat of arms? Perhaps you should add it to the arms when you inherit."

Walker laughed. "That is indeed the very cutlass. Father was not pleased with the purchase and insisted it was too dangerous a toy for a child my age. Mother suggested we hang it where it is now until I was old enough. I was off to Eton not long after that, and then I was off to sea where cutlasses abound and are not toys at all."

"Indeed. And stop me if I'm prying, but you referred to your mother as both 'stepmother' and 'mother.'"

"Did I? No, not prying at all. My mother died giving birth to me and Father remarried a year after. My new 'mother' raised me from infancy so, while she is my stepmother, I think of her as my mother."

"But what of you and the sea, Samuel?" Walker asked. "An Irish farmer's son who's no less a seaman than I. How did you come to the sea?"

"Ah, the farming's just done to give us an air of respectability. The money's not in farming. Didn't you know I come from a long and respected line of pirates and smugglers?" Mink said with a grin.

Walker laughed. "Of that I have no doubt, none at all."

"Ah, but there's some truth to that, and thereby hangs a tale."

"Of course," Walker said, and he shifted in his seat a bit to settle back and listen while Darling and Cannon each cocked an ear aft. Mink began, playing to his audience of three.

"It's a story that begins back in the mists of Irish history when the Norsemen were wont to pillage and plunder the Irish. Come springtime a boatload or three would come ashore, ravage the countryside, and make off again. On occasion, one or two might be left behind, having gotten wounded or lost their way and been captured. Most of these were put to the sword, but a few managed to survive and were assimilated.

"As the story is told in my family, one of these fellows, Minke by surname, but spelled then with a final 'e', was spared because he was so wonderfully manly and attractive that the women of the village where he was captured begged the men not to slay him but to spare his life if he would foreswear his barbarian ways. He was, it was said, found in truth to be a good man, kind of heart, and deeply regretful of the harm he had caused. He was also certainly possessed of a great deal of common sense for, when faced with the choice of the sword or assimilation, he readily agreed to abandon his outlaw roving and settle in the village.

"Now, being so manly and attractive, it was only natural that all the young women of the village sought him out for their husband, and only natural that he might choose the most beautiful and intelligent of them for his wife."

His audience had seen this coming and broke into appreciative laughter as Mink sat up and, with a broad grin, concluded, "And as I am sure you have certainly divined by now, I trace my heritage directly to this handsome couple, having lost only the final 'e' of that heritage over the years."

As the carriage turned a final corner and stopped in front of White's, Walker said, "So then, we have explained both your seagoing and, along the way, the reason an Irishman bears the unlikely name of Mink."

Cannon held the door as they stepped down. Walker spoke again, "That will be all for today, men. We may be late, so we'll hire back."

A few people on the street marveled at the odd site of two sailors in charge of a landau as it departed, and Walker and Mink walked to the door. When they entered the club, an attendant approached them, bowed and took their hats.

"Good evening, Commander."

"Good evening, Diggs. Diggs, this is my particular friend, Lieutenant Mink. The Lieutenant will be staying with me for the foreseeable future."

Diggs bowed to Mink and said, "Welcome lieutenant. At your service, sir," before disappearing with their hats.

White's was popular with naval officers and a number of them were present that night.

"Before we eat, what do you say we try our hands at whist?" Walker said.

"An excellent thought," Mink replied. Mink's ease with numbers made him a formidable card player and, after vingt et un, whist was his game. They entered a room where whist was being played, and a naval captain stood from a table across the room, motioning to Walker.

As they approached the table, the captain took Walker's hand and said, "Hello, Walker. We're in need of two for whist. Are you both game?"

"We are, James," Walker replied, "with pleasure."

The officer was James Colins. Walker had served under him when he was fourth lieutenant on the *Indefatigable* and Colins was the first. Colins, who had been a captain for some years, greeted Walker effusively. "By God, it's good to see you, Albert. And look at that fresh swab on your shoulder. We'll have to wet that straightaway."

Colins referred to the custom of toasting an officer's promotion by drinking a toast to the swab, a sailor's slang for epaulette.

"Thank you, James. It's good to see you again. And this is my good friend, Samuel Mink"

Colins extended a hand. "My great pleasure, lieutenant." He turned to the other officer at the table. "May I present John Acton. John, my friend and comrade, Albert Walker, and lieutenant Samuel Mink."

They all shook hands and made appropriate noises. Acton and Colins sat across from each other. Walker took a seat across from Mink.

As Colins picked up the cards, he signaled to a passing waiter to bring another bottle of wine. Colins then shuffled the cards, spread them face down on the table, and turned up a card, the Jack of diamonds. Acton pulled out a ten of hearts, Mink drew the eight of clubs. Walker turned up the six of hearts.

"So it's John and I against you and Samuel, and it's our deal, Albert," Colins said as the waiter arrived with the fresh bottle and refilled their glasses.

Colins was the senior at the table. He raised his glass to Walker. "To your promotion, commander." They drank that toast and another as Colins added, "To the King." It was customary to stand while toasting the King, but naval officers were privileged to remain seated because, according to legend, William IV had struck his head on a deck beam while rising to receive a toast at a shipboard dinner and had decreed that naval officers, for ever after, were privileged to sit while toasting their monarch.

Walker, who sat to Acton's left, shuffled the cards and placed the deck before Acton. Acton dealt and Colins began the play. It was considered bad form to comment on the cards in whist so, as play progressed, the small talk at the table naturally centered on the Navy. After Walker was coaxed to retell his taking of the French ship, during which he insisted that Mink relate his part in the action, talk drifted to the prospects of a renewed war with France.

The four men at the table all stood to gain from a war. England funded her military well in time of war but neglected it sadly during times of peace. Regiments dwindled in size and fleets were laid up in ordinary. Naval officers not assigned to a ship received only half their pay. Without a war there was no way for a naval officer to advance in rank and no opportunity to share in the prize money earned from the sale of a captured ship.

Acton was optimistic, "I say we're months away from it, if that. Boney only agreed to peace because we were getting the best of him. The politicians just mucked it up, gave him a chance to regroup and rearm, and that's just what he's been doing, building ships and raising armies. Mark my words, war's coming soon. What say you, James?"

Colins played a card to the trick. "I can't disagree with you, John," he said. "I too, think the peace was a bad idea and it's just going to give us more work to do when it ends. We should have finished the job."

Acton played a card, took the trick and led a spade. Colins continued, "And, from what I glean from Whitehall, we soon will be at it again. There's a great deal of paper being pushed about up there, and quite a few ships have already been brought out of ordinary and are being refitted. But the thing that convinces me most is that privateers are starting to fit out. When private money's being put at risk, you know something's afoot, and here it's war with France."

Walker studied his hand a moment and played a card. He was content to listen, but Colins drew him in.

"What can you add to this, Albert?"

"Me? I know little of this. But I agree that war seems near and, if privateers are fitting out, nearer than I thought."

The conversation drifted away from war, and play continued for a few more rubbers until Colins and Acton begged off, claiming other obligations.

As Acton began to total the score, Mink said, "I believe we were six rubbers up on you and, figuring honors, that should put our winnings at ten pounds, six."

Acton looked up at Mink, then continued his totaling. Finished, he said to Mink, "Amazing, you had it exactly. How did you do that?"

Walker spoke, "Samuel has an amazing head for figures. The first time we worked a sight together, he had worked the position in his head before I was done writing down the numbers. I thought I had him because, when I finished writing it out on paper, I had a different outcome. He took a quick glance at my work and showed me the error in my figuring. I've never questioned him since."

"Extraordinary," Acton said to Mink. "How did you learn that?"

Mink laughed. "Oh. It's nothing learned. It's just something I've always been able to do. I was quite surprised when I found that everyone couldn't do it."

"Well, I certainly can't," Acton said. "Truth be told I'm a bit daunted still by working out a noon sight."

As he stood, Colins added, "You are not alone, John, I assure you. In fact, I am a bit daunted by any of the mathematics."

As Colins and Acton said their goodbyes, Colins said to Walker, in an aside, "I caught a glimpse of you at the Admiralty, today, Albert. Just a word. It's been my experience that things there may not always be what they seem."

"Thank you, James," Walker replied. "I should not doubt it."

As Colins and Acton walked away, Colins' words recalled to Walker his father's admonition that there is always a wheel we cannot see turning within the one we do.

Walker and Mink stayed on to eat some cold meats and cheese that Mink enjoyed with a good brandy and Walker with coffee.

V I

The next morning, at almost exactly ten o'clock, Darling brought the carriage to a stop in front of Dr. Pearce's Hospital and Asylum, a large four-story brick building. It differed from the others near it in that its windows were covered by iron bars and the building itself was surrounded by a high, spike-topped iron fence in front and a high brick wall around the garden in the rear. A carefully kept lawn separated the building from the fence.

Walker and Mink stepped down from the carriage and walked to the gate; it was locked. Mink rang the bell on the gatepost. Nothing. After he rang a second time, a panel in the center of the door on the front of the building opened and a large round bald head appeared. The eyes squinted suspiciously at them from under remarkably large and bushy eyebrows, cocked to one side but said nothing.

"I am Commander Walker. This is Lieutenant Mink. Dr. Pearce is expecting us."

The head straightened, looked them up and down. The panel closed, they heard a key turn in a lock and, as the door opened, the head reappeared on the broad shoulders of a heavily built man in a short black coat and breeches. He walked through the door, turned, locked it behind him, and plodded down the steps and along the gravel path to the gate. In one hand he carried a large brass ring that held possibly a dozen keys. When he got to the gate, he stood and began to go through the keys one by one until he stopped to examine one more closely. Satisfied, he used it to unlock one of the two locks that secured the gate. He then repeated his search of the keys until he found the one that opened the second lock. Still without speaking, he swung the gate wide and motioned them toward the house. He then carefully locked the gate again before following them to the door to the house and unlocking it. Once inside, he locked the door behind them and led them to a large reception room.

In a voice so deep that it could almost be felt as well as heard he said, "Please, be comfortable. I will let the doctor know you are here." With that, he bowed, turned, and left the room.

Walker spoke first. "You know, Samuel, I believe that his is the first time I have ever been someplace where one needed a key to get out."

"I only wish I could say the same," Mink replied.

Walker looked at him surprised. "You, Samuel?" he said.

"Oh. It was some time ago, wild oats and that sort of thing. It only happened once or twice, twice at the most. The local constabulary and I had a difference of opinion on what constituted an enjoyable evening on the town. I was their occasional guest until we could see eye to eye, generally by the next morning."

Walker's laughter was cut short by the entrance of a small, intense, formally dressed man who began talking rapidly even before he got through the door.

"Good morning gentlemen. It's so good of you to call. You must have heard about the bees, about their having come back. They're a bit late, of course, and that did give me concern, but they're here now and seem to be in fine fettle. Not like last year, oh, that was so distressing, wasn't it? But we managed to cheer them up, and all was well. Would you like to see them? You really must, and they will be so happy that you stopped by. Come along. We can talk on the way then, right this way." The little man turned toward the door, but, before Walker and Mink could begin to follow him, a tall, thin man, dressed like the one who had let them in, appeared in the doorway.

"Ah, there you is, Mr. Willerby. There you is. We's been lookin' all over for ye we has Mr. Willerby. Come along then, yer bees is missing you something terrible, they is."

"They are? Oh dear."

"Yes, Oh dear's the word, Mr. Willerby, all sad and such they is without ye, sad and such for sure, for sure, sir."

"Oh, we'd best go then. You gentlemen must excuse me, but I'm sure you understand."

"Quite," Walker replied, with a bow.

The orderly put one arm around the little man's shoulders and began to lead him away.

"Of course they does, Mr. Willerby, of course they does. Come along now, come along."

As they disappeared down the hall, Walker and Mink looked at each other and shrugged. Mink began to speak, but stopped when another man appeared, well-dressed and balding, with a hint of absentmindedness about him. Peering through spectacles he wore at the end of his nose, he extended a hand to Walker, bowed slightly, and introduced himself.

"Good morning, commander. I am Dr. Pearce." He pronounced it 'purse'.

"Good morning, doctor," Walker replied, taking his hand. "And this is my good friend and colleague in this matter, Lieutenant Samuel Mink. Lieutenant Mink has my full confidence."

"How do you do, lieutenant," he said with a bow to Mink.

"Please accept my apologies for Mr. Willoughby's interruption. He's quite harmless and, for most of the time, a respected academic. Periodically, however, he insists that he's being visited by an apparently congenial swarm of bees. It takes me a week or so to dissuade him of this illusion, after which he is quite normal for a year or so. Curious case, is it not?"

Pearce straightened, "But you are here about Captain Jenkins, not Mr. Willoughby's bees. Perhaps we should start off by visiting the captain, then we can repair to my chambers to discuss his case?"

"As you suggest," Walker replied. Mink nodded in agreement.

"Before we see him, I should tell you what to expect. Won't you have a seat?" He pointed to several chairs by a window. As they sat, he began.

"Captain Jenkins was brought to me unconscious, wrapped in blankets, but still dangerously cold. I had him placed before a large fire and set the attendants to rubbing his limbs. It took some time, but he finally came around, though he was far from his senses."

"What do you mean by 'far from his senses?'" Mink asked.

"Well, at first, he looked about him, apparently without seeing us. He looked beyond us, as it were. Then he tried to jump up, and when we restrained him, he began to call out loudly, saying, as I recall--it's in my notes, but, as I recall," Pearce looked up to the ceiling and scratched his chin for a moment. "Ah, yes, he said things like, 'vast there,' 'haul away,' and he demanded someone stop 'in the name of the King.' He then went silent, staring absently once again, and he seemed to sleep. We dressed him in warm clothes and restrained him in a bed."

"Has he improved at all? Is he still restrained?" Walker inquired.

"He has improved to the extent that he no longer has to be restrained. We cleaned up his clothes and he seems to be more at ease in a uniform coat, but he still seems unaware of where he is, and he has occasional delusional outbursts."

"Delusional outbursts?" Mink asked.

"That's what I call them. He will be completely calm, sitting in his room, eating in the commons, when he stops, appears to look off in the distance, crouches defensively all of a sudden, then turns back with a look of horror over his face, as if he's witnessing some tragedy. He cries out, tears streaming, and he covers his eyes and sobs aloud, finally collapsing. We carry him to his bed where he sleeps for a bit and then awakes and goes on as none of it had happened."

"Is there anything about these episodes that suggest he's in a storm at sea? It was a storm at sea, he has said, that took his ship during a naval battle. Or has he said anything about a naval battle during these episodes, about being chased by a ship?" Walker asked.

"Nothing of that sort that I am aware of and nothing my attendants have reported to me, but I shall ask of them."

"Do you recall if he says anything during these episodes beside what you told us?" Walker asked. "I feel it may be important."

"Not that I recall. If he did, it will be in my notes. Do you have any other questions before we see the captain?"

"Not I," from Walker.

"Nor I," from Mink.

"Let us go then. You may speak to him, but do not be surprised if he does not acknowledge you."

They stood and followed Dr. Pearce down a long hallway in the center of the building. As they passed a stairwell, they heard the high-pitched peals of a woman's laughter coming from somewhere in the floors above. They were cut short by the slamming of a door. Walker and Mink instinctively walked closer to each other. They followed the doctor into a smaller hallway on the left. He stopped at a door, took a key from his waistcoat pocket and opened it.

The room contained a bed, a washstand, and a table with paper, writing instruments and a Bible on it. A convenience sat in the corner. Captain Jenkins, in uniform, sat in an upholstered chair, staring out the room's only window.

"Captain Jenkins, I have brought visitors," Pearce began. Jenkins did not react. He continued to stare out the window.

As Pearce continued to speak to Jenkins, Mink walked to the table. He saw that Jenkins had been writing. One piece of paper caught his eye. On it Jenkins had written a series of numbers. As Mink picked it up to read it, Jenkins gaze shifted to Mink. He stared at him momentarily, then jumped to his feet, knocking his chair over. His eyes fixed on Mink, he lunged, arms extended.

Walker looked at Mink, both men tensed and watched Pearce go after Jenkins. But before Pearce reached him, Jenkins pounced toward Mink.

"Damn you!" Jenkins shouted as Mink dropped the piece of paper, stepped to his left, grabbed Jenkins' left arm and spun him to the right, flinging him down on his back on the bed and pinning him there with his weight. Walker joined him as Pearce opened the door and blew a silver whistle taken from his waistcoat pocket. Two orderlies rushed into the room and relieved Walker and Mink of the struggling Jenkins.

While the orderlies restrained Jenkins, Pearce urged from the hall, "Come outside, gentlemen, please."

As they left the room, Mink stooped to pick up the paper with the numbers on it and put it in his pocket.

"I'm so sorry," Pearce said as they stood in the hall. I had no idea he'd act that way. He's never been violent with anyone while he's been here."

"It's quite all right," Walker replied, "It may have been our uniforms that upset him."

"Or he might have mistaken me for someone," Mink added.

"Yes, yes," Pearce added, "something about you disturbed him deeply. But come along now to my private chambers, will you? I have all my notes there, and we will be more comfortable, I'm sure."

Dr. Pearce's chambers were in the rear of the building. It was a large comfortable room, lined with bookshelves that held academic works and patient files. The doctor's desk and a table behind it were piled with papers. Papers tied with ribbon. Papers in folders. Papers of several sizes, lying as loose single sheets, all spread out with no apparent rhyme or reason. It occurred to Walker that Admiral Burns' desk, though also piled high with paper, showed signs of organization. There was nothing about Dr. Pearce's desk and table that suggested any rational design.

Windows on the rear wall overlooked a formal garden. Walker watched an attendant lead several patients into the garden, each ignoring the others. One young man left the group, walked up to a tree and began to hit his forehead against it. When the attendant tried to stop him, he ran away, flapping his hands rapidly. None of the others showed any reaction. Pearce and Mink joined Walker by the window.

"If I am confident that a patient will not harm himself or others, I permit them time to wander in the garden. I believe it has a calming influence."

"But was not the young man doing himself some violence," Mink observed.

"Ah, yes, he lives in his own world, unable to communicate with anyone. He will do that to himself periodically no matter where he is. I keep hoping that the garden will draw him out."

The doctor motioned to two large, comfortable-looking armchairs that faced his desk. "Please, take a seat. Would you care for coffee?"

Walker looked at Mink, who nodded assent. "Yes, thank you," he replied. Dr. Pearce pulled a bell cord near the door and walked behind his desk.

"But you want to know about Captain Jenkins. I have my notes right here," he said as he reached toward the table behind him.

Walker expected the doctor to rummage around a bit in the mess on the table. Instead, his hand dove confidently into the sea of paper and surfaced with a handful of handwritten notes that he placed in a small clearing in the piles on his desk. He shuffled through them briefly before reaching behind himself, without looking, to submerge his hand once again to retrieve one more piece of paper.

As he arranged the papers, the attendant who had let them in appeared in the doorway and cocked his head to one side.

"Ah, George," Pearce said, "coffee for us, if you will." George bowed and left the room.

Pearce began, "There is much I can tell you about the captain, but perhaps it will simplify things if you tell me what it is that brings you here."

Walker leaned forward and replied, "As I'm sure you know, the captain lost his ship, allegedly in a storm while being chased by a larger French vessel. At least this was the explanation he and the other survivors gave to the court martial, and which the court accepted. But this attack on Jenkins has cast some doubt on the truth of what was said there. We've come to see what you might be able to tell us that would shed some light on those suspicions."

Pearce looked out the window and gently scratched his chin as he considered the question. Before he could answer, George appeared with the coffee. He poured three cups, passed one to each of them and, leaving the pot on a table behind them, left the room.

"Thank you, George." Pearce's words followed the attendant as he closed the door behind him.

Mink began to reach for the flask inside his waistcoat, but a glance from Walker stopped him.

Pearce took a sip of coffee and began. "I have treated a number of soldiers who have been in battle and come away with no physical wounds but with severe defects of mind. These defects appear to manifest themselves in a reliving of the events, a harkening back to a time of great stress. Like Jenkins, the men appear to relive the event that gave rise to their affliction. But, in all other cases, they have lived quite normal lives in between the episodes of reliving."

He shuffled briefly through his notes and continued.

"Jenkins' case differs from the others, though, in that neither I nor anyone else on staff has ever seen your captain appear to be living in the present, in recognition of where he is, or of what is happening around him. I suspect that this is because the shock of his experience in the water has caused a form of catatonia in him, which has caused him to quite withdraw."

Walker interjected, "You said that, during these episodes, he turns away and crouches down, then turns back and looks off in the distance with an expression of horror. Do you think that his behavior arises from what he experienced when he lost his ship?"

"It is possible, but without knowing more of his history or being able to communicate the way I do with others, it would be difficult to say with any assurance. And, of course, I am no sailor, so I have no idea of what one experiences on a sinking ship."

Walker again. "Of course. And in your notes, you were going to see if he said anything during these episodes."

Pearce shuffled through the notes again. "No, he appears to have said nothing."

Walker turned to Mink. "Samuel, what questions do you have for the doctor?"

Mink held up the paper he had taken from Jenkins' room. "What can you make of this, doctor? I realize now that I was looking at it when he set on me." He handed the paper to Pearce.

"Oh, yes, the numbers," Pearce said. "We found a paper with these numbers on it closely folded in an inner pocket of his uniform coat. The numbers were quite faded but just readable. We dried it out and placed it back in the coat before we dressed him in his uniform again. This appears to be a fresh copy he has made. I imagine now that that is what could have caused him to assault you." He looked from Mink to Walker. "I should return this to him. I'm afraid it will overly unsettle him to be without it."

"Of course," Mink said. "But may I make a copy first?"

"By all means." Pearce replied. He indicated a writing desk by the window. "Use that desk there."

Mink took a swallow of coffee and walked across the room as Walker sat forward and addressed Pearce. "So, doctor, is it safe to say that Jenkins is suffering from two shocks to his mind: the loss of his ship, no matter how it happened, and the incident that brought him here? And that these shocks manifest consistently in those acting-out incidents that you describe?"

"In a broad sense, yes, with the caveat that I know nothing of his life other than those two events. But it is, yes, safe to say that those two events are what plague his mind and express themselves as I have described."

"Thank you, doctor. I see that my colleague has finished copying the paper, so we should take our leave. Your time is valuable, and we have spent much of it."

Walker rose to leave. Mink handed the paper to Pearce and put the copy in his pocket.

Pearce pulled the bell rope, and George met them as they entered the hallway. "I will walk you to the door, and George will see you through the gate."

They walked the length of the building and took their leave of the doctor as George again went through the ritual of unlocking the front door and then examining his keys to find the correct ones to open the gate. They thanked him and stepped into the carriage.

As they drove off, Mink asked, "Do you possibly have any charts at the house, of the West Indies, say?"

"I do. I purchased charts of my voyages to show to my mother and sister. But what do we need of charts? Something you saw in those numbers, eh?"

"Precisely. I believe Jenkins' numbers may be a crude cypher for latitude and longitude."

V I I

Back at the house, Walker led the way to the library where several charts sat rolled up on a high shelf. Walker took them down and unrolled them until he found one that covered a portion of the West Indies. He handed it to Mink.

"Will this suit?"

Mink unrolled it on a table and scanned it quickly.

"Quite well," he said as he secured it open with candlesticks placed at the corners. "And would it tax you to produce parallel rules?"

"Not in the least," Walker said. He opened a drawer under a shelf of books and produced a set.

Mink took the paper onto which he had copied Jenkins' numbers out of his pocket and studied the first set.

"So,' he said, "Divide the first line by two, and we get 21 degrees, 11 minutes, and 52 seconds north. From the second line, I get 71 degrees, 37 minutes, and 51 north."

"Divide a seven digit number by two," Walker repeated, "in your head? You never cease to amaze me with your grasp of numbers"

Mink grinned, "Simple enough."

Walker shook his head as Mink took a pencil and, using the parallel ruler, quickly located the position and scratched a small x on the chart.

Walker leaned over the chart. "It appears you have found a spot of open water."

"Yes," Mink said, "Not what I had hoped for, but not surprising. It is not unknown for the Admiralty to misplace the occasional island, and I am sure there are many small islands not dreamt of in their philosophy, Horatio."

"Indeed, my prince, indeed," Walker replied to complete Mink's allusion. Looking up from the chart, Walker continued, "But if, as the survivors testified, the *Diligence* sank in the Atlantic, what is the significance of this spot?"

"An excellent question," Mink replied. "But Jenkins seemed terribly upset that we came upon it. And what if she didn't go down in the Atlantic? We already have serious doubts about how she went down; why should we not doubt where she disappeared?"

"And then again, this spot may signify something else entirely."

"Yes, but I think we can safely assume that the ship was at this position at some time in her voyage and that she did not sail directly home from Jamaica," Mink suggested, looking to the doorway where Jessup had just appeared. "But let us consider it over dinner."

During their meal, they decided that their next stop was to be the dockyard at Woolwich, just downriver from London, where Jenkins had been assigned and where he was found under the pier. They sent Darling with a message requesting an appointment with the superintendent, who responded that he would be pleased to receive them any day during the week.

VIII

Two days later, Walker, Mink, Darling and Cannon walked into Clock House, the administration building at Woolwich. Cannon and Darling stopped just inside the door as Walker and Mink approached a clerk.

"I am Commander Walker. This is Lieutenant Mink. The superintendent is expecting us."

"Ah yes," the clerk replied. "This way please." He led them up an open flight of stairs to a room on the second floor. The door was open.

"Commander Walker and Lieutenant Mink, sir," the clerk said, stepping aside to let them in.

"Thank you, Taylor."

Taylor bowed slightly and closed the door behind him. Captain Dooley, the superintendent, sat behind a desk that was completely empty save for an inkwell and quill, not a piece of paper, not a journal. Nothing. At his back was a large window that overlooked the yard. On the opposite wall stood a sideboard with several decanters and glasses. Paintings of ships hung on the walls. Dooley was short, thin, and balding. What hair he had left was pure white and pushed haphazardly back over his ears. He wore a uniform coat and neck cloth. A black patch covered his left eye.

"Welcome, gentlemen. Please take a seat. Would you care for anything to drink?"

As they sat down, Mink looked to Walker who replied, "Not for me, thank you," and looked to Mink.

"Nor I, thank you."

Dooley began the conversation, "So, you've come about Jenkins. What can I do for you?"

Walker began, "We'd like to see where he was found, and we were hoping to speak with these men." He handed a piece of paper to Dooley on which he had written the names of five of the men who had survived with Jenkins and who had been working at Woolwich. Dooley turned his good eye to the paper and scanned the list.

"Holdsworth is still here, at work in the wood shop. Watkins quit soon after the incident with Jenkins, and the other three are deceased."

"Deceased?" Mink repeated.

"Deceased," Dooley said. "They died in accidents here in the yard."

"All three? Of one group? Isn't that a bit unusual?" Mink asked.

"Oh, no doubt," Dooley replied. "After the third death I went back and examined the others, but there was nothing obvious about them that would cause me to say they could not be accidents."

A clerk knocked at the door and entered. He placed several pieces of paper on the desk before Dooley.

"Excuse me, won't you?" Dooley moved quickly through the papers, signing letters and making notes in the margins of the others before handing them back to the clerk and leaving the desk once again clear.

After the clerk left, Dooley said, "Here, why don't we talk on our way to wharf where they found Jenkins. We'll have no interruptions that way." As they stood, Dooley opened the top drawer of his desk, took out a key and placed it in his waistcoat pocket. They went down the stairs. Darling and Cannon joined them, and they set off through a door in the back of the building that led into the yard itself. The ways were filled with ships in various stages of refitting. The forges, the rope walk, and all the other shops were in full operation. Piles of timber of all sizes dotted the yard.

"The wharf where he was found is one on the upriver side of us," Dooley said as he led the way.

Walker asked, "What can you tell us of his duties here? Who did he work with who might have wanted to harm him?"

Dooley led them around a pile of chain. "I should have an easier task to list those who would not wish him some harm, but I can think of no one that would actually inflict it. I'll be honest. He was a most unpleasant individual, but his faults were not the sort of thing for which you'd kill a man. They sent him to me to keep him off half pay, a sinecure. Sent me those men you listed. We found good employment for the men, and I made Jenkins one of my assistants with the tacit understanding that he was to do nothing unless he was asked."

They stopped as a team of horses noisily dragged a large timber across the path they were on.

As it passed, Dooley continued, "The position required him to do little or nothing. Any decent man would have recognized his good fortune and stayed out of the way, but not Jenkins. He began nosing about, issuing orders, finding fault, and currying favor. I had to speak to him several times, but it did little good. So I, for one, am pleased to have him gone, but certainly not the way it happened."

They walked under the bowsprit of a third rate in its dock and approached a line of warehouses built out over the river. They walked along them until Dooley stopped at one, took the key from his waistcoat pocket, and unlocked the padlock that secured it. He stepped back and motioned to Darling and Cannon to open the door. Iron wheels complained along the iron track as noisily for them as they had for the man in the boat cloak as the door yielded.

"You'll find the cage and the hole in the floor about halfway down. And you'll lock up after?" Dooley said.

"Of course." This from Walker. "And do you mind if we stop and see you on the way out if we have more questions?"

"Not in the least. You should find me at the top of the stair."

Dooley turned and walked back into the yard as the four men entered the warehouse. Their eyes adjusted slowly to the dim light shining in through the cracks between the boards that formed the walls of the building. They could just make out the shape of the cage lying on its side next to a hole in the floor. Two boards had been pried loose in the process of freeing Jenkins from it.

"Must have been a right horror to have been hanging in that thing as the tide rose around you," Mink said. "Cold, wet and waiting to drown."

"Indeed," Walker agreed, "It's no surprise he came a bit unhinged."

They looked at the scene for moment or two until Walker continued, "Whoever did it was someone who could move about the yard without raising any suspicions, but it was still a nice trick to sneak the cage in here."

"Beg pardon, sir," Darling injected, "but 'e could 'ave brought it in in pieces, cobbled it up in 'ere. Who's the wiser about some bloke carrying boards 'bout a shipyard?"

"Specially if he's a carpenter," Cannon added. "Look how careful the work is. Boards is cut careful to length, edges chamfered, corners rounded. The man who built this is used to doin' it right."

Mink knelt down to get a closer look. "He's right, Albert. This is good work carefully done."

"By a carpenter, is it?" Walker replied. "And our man Holdsworth is at work here in the wood shop. If we've seen enough here, shall we pay him a visit?"

Walker turned to Darling and Cannon. "Seen enough, men?"

"Aye," Darling replied as Cannon nodded.

"Then let's lock up and find the wood shop."

Walker led the way as they retraced their steps to the door. Darling pushed it shut, and Cannon snapped the lock closed in the hasp.

As they regained the yard proper, Walker stopped and looked around. "Where do you suppose the wood shop is?"

Mink hailed a workman on a scaffold on the side of a ship. "You there, where away's the wood shop?"

The man pointed up the path in front of the docks. "Up that end it is, beyond the docks and just before the rope walk."

"Thank you," Mink said with a slight nod of his head.

"Aye," the man replied with a knuckle to his brow.

The carpentry shop was bathed in the warm smell of sawdust and wood shavings. Several men were working there. One was fashioning deadeyes, the wood blocks that standing rigging was rove through to adjust it. Two were assembling a hatch grating, a man in the rear was putting the finishing touches on an oar, and another one was sweeping up. They entered the shop and approached the sweeper.

Mink said, "We are looking for John Holdsworth."

The others looked up as the sweeper pointed to the man working on the oar. "At's 'im, at the oar."

The man at the oar kept working as they walked to the back of the shop.

Walker asked, "Are you John Holdsworth?"

Holdsworth felt along the blade of the oar and removed a small sliver of wood with a spokeshave before, still intent on his work, he replied, "I am." He sighted along the blade and felt it one more time before he turned to Walker and said, "What do you want of me?"

The others kept at their work but strained to listen as Darling and Cannon nosed about the shop.

Walker replied, "We have come about Captain Jenkins. Are you are aware of what happened to him?"

"Aye, everyone 'ere is. Someone 'ung 'im under a pier, left 'im for dead." He turned back to the oar, pulled another small strip of wood from the blade and ran his hand over it again.

"And we're trying to find out why that happened. We think it may have to do with the loss of the *Diligence* so we're talking to all the survivors. We hoped you might be able assist us."

"I know naught of it but that he was 'ung there."

"Do you know of anyone who might have wanted to do this?"

"I don't. 'E wasn't loved by 'is crew, but 'e weren't the worst. Somebody must 'ave 'ad it in for 'im, but it weren't me."

"What can you tell us of the leaving of the ship? Did anything happen there or on the passage back to Jamaica that might have raised a resentment?"

"Nay. We was all hands at getting the launch afloat and away."

"And the cutter," Mink added.

Holdsworth hesitated slightly, "Aye, the cutter, too. All like I said to the court."

He released the oar from the vise on the workbench, ran his hands along the length and, satisfied, laid it with several other new oars. From a stack next to that, he picked up a long, narrow piece of ash with the outline of an oar marked on it in charcoal, placed it in the wood vise, and picked up a drawknife.

As Holdsworth pulled the first shaving off the ash blank, Walker asked, "One more thing. Everything said to the court related to the attack by the Frenchman and your escape. Nothing was said about the course to the attack. Did the ship stop at any land on the way out? Or did the launch on the way back?"

Holdsworth again hesitated a fraction of a second before replying. "Nay. We was straight out of Jamaica and then back." A second long thin strip of ash fell to the floor as Walker looked to Mink and raised his eyebrows.

Mink nodded toward the door.

Walked turned back to Holdsworth, "Thank you, Holdsworth, you've been most helpful. We won't keep you from your work any longer. Good day."

"Good day, sirs," Holdsworth said and managed a knuckle to his forehead before he returned to shaping the oar.

They stepped back into the sunlight and began to walk to the administration building.

Walker spoke first, "Well, Samuel, what think you of John Holdsworth?"

"I think he's a poor liar. I think he knows all of what happened to Jenkins, and, more than ever, I think there's a lot more to know about the loss of the *Diligence*."

"And there's this, sir," Darling said as he reached into his jacket and produced a piece of wood. "Found this back of the workbench. Looks to be sawn off one of the boards as made the cage. Same width and chamfered just like."

Walker took it from him and stopped. He turned it over in his hands and handed it to Mink. "Samuel?"

Mink examined it briefly and handed it to Cannon. "Darling's right. It's of a piece with one of the planks."

"So Holdsworth is our man. What do we do with him?"

"Nothing. It is our task to find out what happened and the Admiralty's to do something about it. Come, let us thank Dooley and get on our way. I think we know enough now to report to Admiral Burns, don't you?"

"I do."

When they returned to Walker's house, they went to the library where Walker took some sheets of paper from a drawer and put out an inkwell and quills.

"What do you say, Samuel, if I outline what we know of Jenkins and Holdsworth, and you write up what you think of the numbers we took from Jenkins. When we're done, we'll combine it in a fair final draft."

Mink nodded agreement and picked up a quill.

45

In their completed report, they concluded that the testimony before the court martial was, if not a complete fabrication, at best incomplete, and that the ship had not sailed directly from Jamaica out into the Atlantic as the witnesses had claimed. Instead, they speculated that the *Diligence* had made a passage to the vicinity of the location Mink had identified and that the reason for this deviation from her course might have given rise to the attack on Jenkins. They also concluded that the ship's carpenter, Holdsworth, was the person who had made the cage and, lacking contrary evidence, the man who placed Jenkins in it.

When Walker finished reading the final draft aloud to Mink, he asked, "Well Samuel, what do you think?"

"I think you have a way with words almost equal to that of an Irishman, and I think, too, that it may be time for a brandy."

"I will take that as a high compliment, and I will join you in the drawing room as soon as I craft a letter to accompany this."

The following morning after breakfast, Walker sealed the report and letter and called Darling and Cannon to the dining room, "Men, I want you to take this to the Admiralty. You'll be met at the door by a porter. Hand this to him with this coin under your thumb and over the papers so he sees it and simply say, 'For Admiral Burns, with Commander Walker's compliments, if you will.' The coin assures that he will, and promptly. Understood?"

"For Admiral Burns with Commander Walker's compliments, if you will. Aye sir." Darling said as Cannon nodded.

"Very well, then off with you."

The answer to their report came two days later in the form of a letter from Burns in which he requested they wait upon him the day following if it "might be convenient."

I X

The following day found Walker and Mink walking along the gravel path toward the entrance to the spiral stair. At the top Walker knocked twice, hesitated and knocked once. After a few moments, a clerk opened the door and led them into Burns' chambers. The admiral greeted them with a warm smile and firm handshakes.

"Thank you both for coming. Commander, it's good to see you again. And Lieutenant Mink, it's an honor, sir. The *Gazette* served you badly in its telling of the business of the cutting out of that corvette. Your friend here set the record right with me."

Before Mink could reply, the admiral indicated the chairs in front of his desk, "Have a seat, won't you?" While they took their seats, he called to the outer room, "Forbes, some claret please. A decanter and three glasses, if you will."

Burns then sat at his desk where their report was in front of him. "This is very good work in a short time. I thank you for it. I have discussed your work with their lordships and they and I quite agree with your conclusions.

"The way we see it is we have a captain who went off on a frolic of his own, abetted by some of his men. Of those men that we can locate, three die in an accident at a shipyard, two disappear shortly thereafter. Right after that, Jenkins is found as he was and, the last man standing, so to speak, Holdsworth, is apparently the man who did it. So I see my suspicions as confirmed. Something did happen on the way back from Jamaica that was not told to the court, and there has been a falling out about it."

Forbes walked in just then with three glasses and a decanter of wine. As he poured, the admiral continued, "Does that put it in a few words?"

Walker looked at Mink. "It does for me," he said as Mink nodded his assent.

Forbes put the decanter down and gave each of them a glass. When he left the room, Burns took a sip of wine and continued. "So we are left with the question of what happened on the way back from Jamaica. Jenkins can't tell us, and Holdsworth won't. The other players in our little drama are either dead or missing."

Walker interjected, "About Holdsworth, sir. What's to become of him?"

"Ah, yes, Holdsworth. More of him in a moment. The first question we must answer is how do we go about finding out what happened?" He took another sip of claret and turned to Mink, "Tell me lieutenant, what would you do?"

Mink was about to have a swallow of wine. He stopped with his glass in midair. "I, sir?"

Lieutenants were not accustomed to being asked for advice by admirals, and Mink's surprise showed on his face.

"Yes, you. By the way, we were impressed by your theory of the meaning of Jenkins' numbers. That was quite persuasive and, we believe, correct. But tell me, what would you do?"

Mink glanced at Walker but got no help, so he decided to jump in with both feet. "Do, sir? Why I should sail to the spot I identified to see what was there."

Burns smiled, nodded, and turned to Walker. "And you, commander. What would you do?"

Walker sensed that a decision had already been made. He conditioned his answer slightly, "Assuming that we have done all we can here, I would join Lieutenant Mink and sail to the spot he identified."

"Do you think we have done all we can here?" Burns asked.

"I do. I can't believe we'll get any more from Jenkins or Holdsworth, any more that's useful, at least."

Burns stood and paced behind his desk.

"We agree with both of you. There is little more to be gained from interrogating Holdsworth, any more that, as you say, may be useful. Their lordships have decided that the best course to pursue is, as you suggest, to sail to that spot and see what light can be shed on the fate of the *Diligence* from there. Accordingly, they have authorized the fitting out of a ship to accomplish just that purpose."

He stopped, looked out the window a moment, turned and addressed Walker, "I have the pleasure to offer you the command of that ship if you will have it, commander. What say you?"

It was Walker's turn to be taken aback. He looked to Mink and back to Burns, "Sir? But sir, there are others on the list who--"

"I know," Burns cut him short. "It will vex those on the list above you, but there are other postings ready to be handed out and, with war in the offing, there will be more than enough ships to go around. Any animosity toward you will soon be forgotten. It was I who suggested you for the post because of your knowledge of this mission, but their lordships' assent was swift and without dissent, and you have solid backing. So, your answer is yes?"

Without waiting for an answer he went on, "Good, then let us get to the details."

Burns sat down at his desk again and picked up a piece of paper. "Ah, here are my notes."

Walker sat in silence. Things were moving too fast. Mink looked from Walker to Burns and back, wondering what this all might mean to him. He didn't have to wait long to find out. Burns pulled his chair up to the desk and began,

"As far as crew, I assume you'll want our lieutenant here as your first, if that suits the two of you?"

Mink's anxiety disappeared as fast as it came on as Walker looked to Mink and addressed Burns, "I'd have none other, sir."

Mink opened his mouth to speak and, for once at a loss for words, closed it.

Burns smiled at Mink, "As I thought."

Burns put the paper aside and looked directly at Walker, "As to your second, this is an instance where you can do me a service, if you will? I have two things to ask of you."

"Of course," Walker replied.

Burns smiled, nodded to Walker, and continued, "There is a young man, Charles Talbot by name, who was made lieutenant some six months or so before the current peace. He is, by all I know, a very competent young officer. He is also my nephew. I should like to place him with superiors who can afford him a good example and see to his continuing education in the business of being a naval officer. I believe you two are up to the task, and I would be honored if you would have him as the ship's second." He looked to Mink and back to Walker.

"I should be most happy to have him," Walked said. This was, of course the only sensible answer, especially after being given his obvious choice of Mink as his first. It was also a small price to pay for a command, and they all knew that, especially in these times.

Burns took another sip of wine and leaned back in his chair. "As to the second thing, I ask it on behalf of your friend, James Colins. His son, James, Jr., is a midshipman of little experience, but a very capable young man. Colins wondered if he might place him with you. He thinks you will be a good example for the young man to follow."

"Of course, sir. James does me an honor. I should be pleased to have his son with me." It occurred to Walker that Colins must be more deeply involved with the Admiralty than he let on if he were aware of this mission at this early stage.

"Then that's settled. Thank you, commander. I shall send both young gentlemen off in the next day or two so you will find them aboard when you arrive in Portsmouth." Walker had little doubt in his mind that Talbot and Colins were on their way to Portsmouth as they spoke.

Burns continued, "Rounding out the officers, there are two midshipmen already aboard who came to their positions through the usual influence, but I have it on good authority they are capable men."

Walked nodded, "I am sure they are, sir."

Burns picked up another sheet of paper off his desk and peered at it briefly, "And now on to these men of yours, Darling and Cannon. Will they serve as your boatswain and gunner?"

Walker tried again not to show his surprise. He had, of course, been planning to bring them with him, but to have them as two of his warrant officers was a pleasant, unexpected shock. "I can think of none better. But neither has a warrant, sir."

"They will have them presently. Cannon's will be acting because there will be no time for the Board to examine him before you depart. He can attend to that on your return. Their warrants will be with your orders."

How, Walker wondered, did Burns know that he employed Darling and Cannon, no less the fact that they were boatswain and gunner, without warrants? He was reminded of Colins' warning about things not always being what they seemed at the Admiralty and his father's remark about wheels within wheels.

Before he could give it all much thought, Burns sat back with his hands on the arms of his chair and, with a slight smile said, "And you will need a carpenter. I was thinking that Holdsworth might be a fitting addition to the crew, don't you agree?" He spread his arms and smiled, looking from Walker to Mink.

Mink laughed and looked to Walker.

"Holdsworth?" Walker said, then added, with a laugh of his own, "Why, of course. Holdsworth."

Mink joined in. "Of course, who knows more about where we are going than he? But how can he be persuaded to come along?"

"You can leave that to me," Burns said, "but I think the offer of a posting to a ship in a time of peace would be enough to get him aboard willingly, don't you? He'll not know that you are in command, of course, and you will not be expecting him, so it will be coincidence and surprise all around, eh?" Burns said with a wink.

"Coincidence and surprise," Walker agreed.

Burns began to poke about on his desk as he continued, "Your voyage, by the way, is officially a survey mission. Your assignment will be to explore and survey certain islands in the chain close to the spot that lieutenant Mink identified."

He pulled out a piece of paper, squinted at it and went on, "Here we are. They have been in our possession for some time now, and there have been salt pans there for a hundred years before that. For all that we know about the large islands, though, we have paid almost no attention to the smaller ones to the south, so, even though this is somewhat thin gruel for its justification, your voyage should occasion little notice and arouse no suspicion. To bolster its credibility, you will carry a surveyor with you."

He peered at a paper in his hand. "A Jeremiah Hopkins by name. He will travel with an assistant by the name of Fletcher."

Burns stopped, took a sip of wine, looked down at his desk a moment, and began again, "There is, of course, another purpose." He looked up, hesitated a moment and said, "In a word, it is gold."

He had their attention anew. Mink looked at Walker, who spoke first. "Gold, sir?"

Burns smiled, "Gold. You may not find it, and don't count your mission less than a success if you don't, but you are to look for it. Allow me to explain." He stood and paced behind his desk. "During the recent hostilities, a fair amount of gold and silver taken from prizes had accumulated in Jamaica. The plan was to ship it back to England as soon as a fleet large enough to assure its safe passage was available. When that fleet was assembled and the treasure finally moved from safekeeping to shipboard, however, it was found that three small wooden crates containing gold bars were missing. The crates were each about thirty or forty pounds or so. Nothing one man couldn't move. An inventory and a thorough search revealed nothing, so the shipment was sent off and the business kept quiet as the investigation continued. Nothing was ever revealed, and the disappearance remains a mystery."

Burns sat again at his desk.

"Now, Jenkins sailed for England some weeks before the gold was to leave. No one thought to suspect him at the time because there was really no reason to, no obvious connection. My suspicions about Jenkins were aroused when he was found as he was. That's why I revisited the court martial. But, of course, there was nothing there to connect him to the gold, just the suspect testimony that piqued my curiosity. But now, the paper you found on Jenkins and Lieutenant Mink's interpretation of that paper may connect them." Burns nodded an acknowledgement to Mink that Mink returned with a nod and a smile.

"So you think the gold may be on an island in the area Samuel identified?"

"It may. I caution you that this is only speculation, but certain of their lordships believe that your expedition is justified in the hope not only of recovering the gold, but of answering the questions that its disappearance has occasioned. In truth, they are as concerned about how the gold disappeared and who might be responsible as they are about the recovery of the gold itself."

Burns got up again and began to pace. "Now, remember, only a very few people know of the disappearance of the gold, and even fewer know of the true nature of your voyage."

He stopped and, as if to emphasize what he said next, looked directly at them, "Even some of their lordships are not privy to your voyage's true nature, so you must be discreet in how you will conduct yourselves in this. And you will receive some additional guidance with your orders."

Walker again heard his father's caution about wheels within wheels as he replied, "Of course, sir. Without question."

"Good," Burns said. "Enough of that. Now then, as to your ship." Burns sat and picked up another piece of paper from a stack on his right. "She is a spar-decked sixth rate of twenty-two guns, *Barbadoes* by name, now lying at Portsmouth. She's far from new, we took her from the Americans just at the end of that business, but she is well made of seasoned timber and recently had a full refit and re-coppering. As I understand, they are still setting up her rigging, but she should be ready for sea within the month, possibly sooner. She was built on their Chesapeake Bay and is, I am told, like those vessels, fast and easily handled. She was built to carry twenty guns, but somewhere along the way, she acquired long nines fore and aft as chasers." He looked up at both men, smiling, "Well, what do you think?"

Walker replied, "I am a bit fazed by it all, sir. It will take me a while to process. But I am eager to get on with it and, of course, extremely grateful for your patronage."

Burns replied, "I assure you, commander, that you would not have my patronage if I and others here did not have full confidence in you. So it is you, commander, and," nodding to Mink, "you as well lieutenant, who have earned this posting. And you will have a bit of time to process it all. Why don't we say that you are to report to your ship any time within the next ten days? Allowing travel time to Portsmouth, that will give you a few days to prepare and put your affairs to order."

"That's more than ample, sir. Thank you. I doubt we shall need it all."

"Your orders, the warrants, and the other necessary paperwork are being drawn up as we speak. They will be delivered to you by the end of the day tomorrow. Are there any questions?" He looked from Walker to Mink.

They glanced at each other before Walker replied, "No, sir, it all seems quite straightforward."

"Good, Then we are done with business." Burns picked up his glass and turned to Mink, who had been but a spectator all this time, and said, "Lieutenant, you must tell me about the taking of that corvette. The account in the *Gazette* was much too dry and lacking of detail, and the account I took from your friend here was much too modest. I must hear it all from you, if you will."

Mink, of course, would. He took a swallow of claret, leant forward in his chair, and launched enthusiastically into a recounting of the attack on the corvette. As Mink warmed to his task, Walker began to list in his mind all that needed to be done in the days ahead. His seagoing kit would need an overhaul; there was food and drink to secure for his personal larder aboard, and more. Jessup would see to all of that. He would make a list for him, and some of it could wait until he arrived in Portsmouth. And there was the revelation slowly dawning upon him that he had a ship. She was old, but newly fitted, and possibly the smallest in the Navy that he could command, but she was his, with all the lonely majesty and responsibility that settled on a naval officer when he assumed command.

He put aside the nagging question of why he had her and turned his attention again to Mink and Burns. Mink had gotten to the point where he and his party had secured the foredeck and were making their way aft. Mink was embellishing things slightly to his more than appreciative audience, but the truth was suffering no real damage.

When he finally wrapped it up, Burns actually applauded.

"Excellent, sir, excellent. You did the tale justice, and I envy you the adventure." As he said this, he picked up his glass and raised it, "Before you go, a toast to your success." They drank and drank again, "To the King."

Walker and Mink let themselves out and down the spiral stair. At the bottom Mink stopped, took his flask out of his waistcoat, had a pull of brandy, shook himself, and said to Walker, "Tell me that we have a ship, that what just happened actually happened."

Walker laughed. "We have a ship, Samuel. I'm as surprised and confused as you, but yes, we have a ship. So, let us make haste, there's much to be done," he said as they took to the gravel path.

X

The door swung open at their approach. As they handed their hats to Jessup, Walker said, "Jessup, the lieutenant and I have been given a ship. We must leave for Portsmouth as soon as we are able. We must make haste; there's much to do."

"Yes sir," he replied. "You'll need your seagoing kit, provisions, servants, and more. There is much to do, indeed."

"Servants. Of course," Walker replied. "I'd forgotten about servants, my young gentlemen."

Captains were permitted a certain number of cabin servants, also known as his young gentlemen. They were usually the sons of family, friends or men of influence. In addition to serving the captain, they would be trained in the nautical arts in preparation for careers in the navy.

"Honestly," he continued, "I can think of no one on such short notice, Samuel. Do you know of any likely candidates?"

"There are likely young men in the family, but all in Ireland, and we'd never get them here in time for us to leave."

Jessup interjected, "If I may be so bold, I may know of suitable candidates, sir,"

Walker turned to Jessup, hesitated a moment, and said, "Very well then. See what you can do."

"I shall see to it, sir. And might I suggest you make a list of your other concerns, and I will compare that to mine?"

"Of course, Jessup, of course."

Jessup turned and left the room. Walker called to the back of the house, "Darling, Cannon, come up here. Great news."

The two men popped out of a doorway at the back of the main hall.

"News, sir?" from Darling.

"Great news. Tell them, Samuel."

Mink beamed, "The commander has been given a ship, and we sail with him, I as his first and you two as boatswain and gunner. We depart in days. What do you think of that?"

Darling and Cannon looked at each other and back at Walker and Mink with blank stares. Confused, Darling replied first, "A ship? Us? As bosun and gunner? That's grand news indeed, sir, but neither of us 'as our warrant."

"And I've to sit for a test 'fore the board to 'ave mine, sir," Cannon added.

"That's all taken care of," Walker assured them. "Your warrants will be delivered in a day or two with my orders. Yours, Cannon, will be acting for this voyage. You can sit the test when we return."

"But what ship, sir? And where are we off to, if I might ask?"

"You may. We have a sixth rate, *Barbadoes* by name, and we're off for the West Indies. We leave as soon as I have my orders and we are ready. But our destination's mum for now, so have a care with it, and make haste."

"Mum it is, and 'aste it is," Darling replied. "We'll be ready to depart any time, and thank you, sir, thank you," he said as he and Cannon headed for the back of the house, again in high spirits.

Walker's orders and the warrants were delivered the following afternoon. Along with the usual order requesting and requiring him to assume command of the *Barbadoes,* there was also a sealed packet marked, "To be opened beyond the 15th meridian of longitude."

There was also a note, in Burns' own hand and under his personal seal, advising them that he had been informed that Jenkins had escaped Dr. Pearce's hospital. He did not think them in any particular danger but thought that they should take whatever precautions they might think advisable. Walker read it and handed it to Mink. They considered the possibility of any danger to themselves and, even considering Jenkins' attack on Mink, dismissed the idea. They reasoned that, even if he were lucid during their visit, all he would know of them were their names, and he certainly would not know how to find them.

X I

The next days were devoted to preparing to spend the next few months at sea.

They did not go to White's the night before they were to leave for Portsmouth, opting instead for supper at home. After they ate, Jessup set out coffee in the drawing room and went off to bed. Mink finished his coffee, put his feet up, and stared into the fire. He was soon asleep, snoring softly.

Walker sat by the fire across from Mink with a chart of the area they were headed for unrolled in his lap. As he studied it, he thought he heard a tapping at the front door. And again, three soft taps. He could hear no one stirring from the back of the house, so he went to the door himself and peered through the glass. He saw only the dark silhouette of a man, cast by the pale light of the street lamp. His body was turned away from the door, looking back onto the street.

"Who is there?" Walker called.

The man turned slightly back toward the house. "Admiralty courier, urgent documents for Commander Walker."

Walker put his hand on the door handle but hesitated. It was late. The Admiralty had closed hours ago. Burns, though, had shown that he had no respect for regular hours. Walker turned the handle. As he began to pull on it, the man turned and pushed the door open, stepping quickly inside. Walker jumped back. The faint light from the few candles in the hallway behind him flickered over his shoulder to reveal Jenkins, standing just inside the door, with a pistol in his hand.

Walker raised his hands in front of himself and took a step back.

"Don't raise an alarm," Jenkins said. "Just show me where it is."

Walker took another step back. "Where what is?" he responded. Another step back. Walker was trying to get to the drawing room, to somehow alert Mink.

"You know full well. The paper you stole from me. I'll have it back. Now."

Walker could see no advantage to denying that they had the paper or explaining that they had left it with Dr. Pearce. Jenkins would never believe him. Walker's best option was to hold Jenkins' attention long enough to alert Mink. He took another step back. Another, hands still open. Jenkins followed Walker as he slowly retreated to the drawing room.

"Where are you going?" Jenkins hissed, waving his gun. "I warn not to try to trick me."

"In here," Walker said. "It's in here."

Walker backed into the room. Jenkins followed, looking cautiously around. The high wingback chair Mink sat in concealed him from Jenkins' view but not from Walker's. Mink had stopped snoring but still appeared to sleep.

Walker raised his voice slightly. "It's here, in the desk behind me, I believe. Put down the gun, and I will get it."

"Get it!" Jenkins demanded, pointing the gun at Walker. "Give it to me. Now. Or I shall take it for myself."

Mink opened his eyes and glanced at Walker. How much, Walker wondered, had he heard? Did he know Jenkins was holding him at gunpoint? Walker quickly got his answer. As Jenkins took aim at Walker, Mink stood suddenly. In one motion, he reached above the fire place, grabbed the cutlass from its place under the coat of arms, and lunged at Jenkins.

Startled, Jenkins swung the pistol toward Mink and fired. The ball caught him in the chest. Mink stopped in midstride and dropped to his knees, then into a heap on the floor.

Walker rushed Jenkins, but Jenkins pulled another pistol from under his coat and aimed it at Walker. The flash and roar caught Walker in midstride. He braced for the impact but felt nothing. Jenkins, he thought, must have missed. Through the smoke, he watched Jenkins spin to his left and fall face forward onto the floor, the pistols slipping from his fingers.

Before Walker could make sense of what had just happened, the silence was broken by Jessup, who walked past him in his nightshirt and cap, carrying a still-smoking pistol.

"Excuse me, sir, but I must see to the lieutenant. I believe you will find that the other gentleman is not seriously wounded."

As they hurried to Mink's aid, Darling and Cannon appeared at the door.

"Keep the servants out and watch him," Walker said, pointing to Jenkins.

Walker and Jessup bent over Mink. "He was hit full in the chest," Walker said while Jessup felt for a pulse.

Just then, Mink opened his eyes and gasped for air. He was alive. Not only was he alive, but there was no blood anywhere on him. There was a large dark stain on his chest, but upon examination, it proved to be brandy. Mink's waistcoat was soaked with it.

Walker knelt down, reached inside the waistcoat, and pulled out Mink's heavy silver flask. Embedded in it was the ball from Jenkin's pistol. The shot had pierced the front of the flask and dented the back, knocking Mink down and taking the wind out of him, but doing no lasting damage. Mink raised his head and looked around.

"What happened? Are you hit?" Mink gasped.

"No, no," Walker replied. "After Jenkins fired at you, he pulled out a second pistol and aimed it at me. But before he could pull the trigger, Jessup walked in and fired a shot that took him down."

Mink laughed, coughed at the pain his chest, and asked, "Jessup? With a pistol? Is there no limit to the man's prescience?" Then looking down at his chest, he added, "And what of me?"

"I expect you're going to have a nasty bruise there for a bit, Samuel, but you will be fine." Holding up the flask, he continued, "But I can't say the same for this gallant flask. I'm afraid it gave its all for you. And I must thank you as well as Jessup. You both saved my life."

"The flask can be replaced, and yours is a life well worth saving, so we both have fared well here. But what of our Jenkins?" he said as he tried to get up. Walker helped him to his feet as they turned their attention to the intruder.

Jenkins lay on his back. Darling and Cannon had turned him over to examine his wound. They had opened his coat and pulled back his shirt.

"Doesn't look bad as pistol wounds go, sir. Not much bleedin', mostly just shocked 'im, I'd think," Cannon said.

Walker knelt down. Jessup's shot had hit Jenkins in the upper chest just under his shoulder. Jessup had been right, it was not a life-threatening wound, disabling surely, but not lethal.

"What are we to do with him now?" Mink asked.

It was then that Jessup walked into the room, tearing a piece of bed linen into strips. "May I suggest that we bind his wound and then bind him? He is going to be quite out of sorts when he comes to his senses."

"Of course," Walker said. "Yes."

Jenkins moaned softly and made as if to sit up as Jessup addressed Darling and Cannon. "Sit him up, won't you? And remove his coat."

Walker and Mink stepped back so that Darling and Cannon could get Jenkins' coat off. They held his arms up and out while Jessup wrapped a few strips of cloth around his chest over a wad of cloth that covered the wound itself. When he had finished tying it off, he handed the rest of the linen to them. "Here, muzzle him and bind his hands and feet."

By the time they had finished this, Jenkins was awake and looking about him with unfocused eyes.

Walker turned to Mink. "You asked what to do with him. What do you say we pay Dr. Pearce another visit? I'm sure he'll be more than pleased to have his patient back, he'll be in a place where he can have his wound looked after, and we'll be well rid of him."

"That's an excellent thought. It will also give me an opportunity to question the good doctor as to the purpose of all his locks and keys and fences and walls and attendants."

Walker turned to Darling and Cannon. "Prepare the landau, and get the enclosure up. It won't serve to drive about town with a bound man in an open carriage."

When the carriage was ready, they carried Jenkins out the back and made their way to the hospital. Lights were on in some of the rooms. Walker rang the bell. No response. He rang it again. On the third attempt the panel opened in the door to reveal the same face that had appeared on their first visit.

"It's Commander Walker. I must see Dr. Pearce, and I must see him now. Fetch him. Make haste."

The panel closed. Several minutes passed before the door opened and Pearce walked out onto the top of the steps. The orderly stood protectively behind him. "Who is there?" he called.

"Commander Walker. I have come to return Captain Jenkins."

Pearce spoke briefly to the orderly, who hurried back into the building. Pearce, holding the ring of keys, hurried to the gate. By the time he had opened the gate, the orderly was back with a colleague.

"Commander I--" Pearce began. Walker cut him off.

"We can talk inside. Jenkins is wounded and bound. He will have to be carried."

The orderlies took the now awake and struggling Jenkins inside the building. He glared at Walker and Mink while Pearce examined his wound in the hallway.

Pearce spoke to the orderlies, "This does not appear overly serious. Take him to my surgery and attend him closely there."

They picked him up and carried him toward the rear of the building.

As Pearce turned toward Walker, Walker pointed down the hallway and spoke angrily, "That man came to my home tonight with two pistols. The lieutenant and I are alive only thanks to Providence and the timely intervention of a trusted servant. We demand to know how that man was at large."

Dr. Pearce's air of detached professionalism was gone. His hands shook slightly as he motioned to chairs in the drawing room. "Sit, please. Allow me to explain, and accept my apologies, please gentlemen."

"We have no time to sit," Walker said, "We leave for Portsmouth within hours. Just tell us how he was at large."

Pearce spoke hesitantly, his voice trembling. "He had seemed much improved in the last few days. He wanted to know what happened to him, to know why he was here. We had several extended conversations, and he was quite lucid. The improvement was so of such a scale and his affect was so improved that I thought a walk in the garden would be therapeutic."

"But he escaped there." Mink finished for him.

Pearce gazed at the floor in front of him. "Yes. My man's attention was diverted for only a moment, and Jenkins was gone. We searched the grounds and buildings to no avail. I informed the Admiralty the very first thing."

"And what of the pistols he carried? Do you keep any weapons here? Are any missing?"

Pearce appeared taken aback. "We have devices to restrain, but none that can do harm."

Walker continued, "And are you still convinced that his earlier condition was genuine and not assumed by him?"

"Yes, I see nothing in what has happened to dissuade me from that."

The conversation paused. Pearce turned as if to leave, then turned back. "Gentlemen, please, if I may see to my patient? And please be assured that he will not have another opportunity to be at large."

Walker could see that there was no point in pursuing the matter further with Pearce. Pearce pulled the bellrope, and the orderly who had let them in appeared with his ring of keys.

"Again, gentlemen, my sincerest apologies. George will see you out," Pearce said. He bowed slightly, turned to walk down the hall, stopped, and turned back. "And if you should have occasion to discuss this with the Admiralty--"

Walker cut him off. "We will say that you did what seemed prudent at the time."

Pearce appeared relieved as he bowed agan, turned, and hurried away.

XII

They were ready to leave the following morning. The hired coach that would take them to Portsmouth arrived just after daybreak. As Darling and Cannon stowed their luggage in the boot, Jessup appeared with two young boys, freshly scrubbed, who looked to be not quite yet in their teens. They, as well as Jessup, were dressed for the road.

Jessup addressed Walker. "May I present Andrew and Arthur. They are nephews of Mrs. Anson. They will assist me as your servants."

The boys made proper bows and stepped back.

Walker said, "Ah, yes, servants. I had almost--" He stopped in mid-sentence and, a bit stunned, turned to Jessup, "Assist you? You are going as my servant?"

Jessup replied calmly. "Why, of course, sir. The boys will need some training and looking after, and who else knows your needs better than I?"

Jessup made it all sound so very obvious that all that Walker could do was to stand there with his mouth open for a second or two before saying, "Very well then, let's get on with it. Make haste."

They filed out the door and boarded the coach. Walker, Mink, Jessup and the boys rode inside. Darling folded up the steps, closed the door, and joined Cannon on the rear box. As the postilion settled into his saddle, the driver picked up the reins and they were off.

The trip to Portsmouth was a tiring series of changes of horses and overnight stays in forgettable inns. Mink found a rapt audience in Andrew and Arthur and entertained them with tales of bloody ship to ship engagements and towering storms at sea. He made it all seem so exciting and romantic that Walker was afraid that the boys would be quite disappointed when they discovered that much of an ocean voyage was dull, quiet, boring routine.

And he wondered about Jessup. Had he been wrong to take him along? From all he knew, Jessup had never been near the ocean, no less sailed on it. Ah, well. If nothing else, he knew Walker's needs well, so it should serve to have him along. Even so, he thought, he would have to keep an eye out for Jessup to see that no misadventure befell him.

They arrived in Portsmouth on the afternoon of the fifth day and put up at the London Inn. As eager as he was to take command, Walker decided to wait until the next day to go on board. From that moment on, he and Mink would be caught up in the unending business of getting the ship ready for sea. At the inn they would have one more day as free men. They would eat well, rest, and collect their thoughts.

After they unloaded the coach and settled into their rooms, Walker paid Darling and Cannon their final wages in his employ, along with a small bonus before they went off to enjoy their last night ashore. Jessup took the boys in tow to "see the sights of Portsmouth." Mink instructed him carefully how to avoid those parts of the city that contained sights unsuitable for young boys.

They chose to eat in a small, private dining room at the inn. A peat fire burned in in a corner fireplace to chase the evening chill.

As they sat down to eat, Mink asked, "So we go aboard in the morning?"

"After breakfast. I sent word to the ship to that effect, to give Talbot a bit of time."

"Fair warning, eh?"

"Aye, that."

They ate in silence for a bit until Walker said, "I'm wondering, Samuel. What do I know about being a master and commander?"

"As much as I know about being a first lieutenant."

Walker laughed.

"But, seriously," Mink added, "it all comes down to leadership, and here's what I think makes a good leader." He ticked the points off on his fingers. "First, you choose good men. Second, you make sure they know what you want them to do, what the job is. Third, you give them the tools and training to do the job. Fourth, be sure they know you'll be there to support them if they need it, and fifth, and probably most important, get out of their way."

"Well said, well said. I shall try to apply that."

"Try to apply it? Why, Albert, you've done that as long as I've known you. True leaders don't have to be shown how to do it. It's a part of them. Where do you think I got my five points? Why, it was from watching you. It is I who have worked to apply them."

"Samuel you flatter me. And you give me some hope for a successful cruise."

"I've never had my doubts about you. Just go on as you have, and you'll do a fine job."

"Thank you, Samuel. Thank you for that."

Walker picked up the decanter. "Would you have more wine?"

"I would, thank you."

As Walker poured, he asked, "It just occurred to me, Samuel, that I have never heard you say 'yes' or 'no.' Just now for instance, I asked if you would have wine, and you said 'I would,' rather than simply 'yes.' Why is that?"

"It's really quite simple," Mink replied. "There are no words for 'yes' or 'no' in the Irish, so we are accustomed to answering with 'I would' or 'I will,' or such. It's simply a habit of phrasing, I guess. It's the way I think in Gaelic and transpose to English, a matter of syntax."

"Fascinating. Do any of the other Gaelic languages have 'yes' and 'no'? The Welsh, the Scots?"

"They do.

"Thank you, Samuel. And what do you think of Jessup coming along as my servant? I was taken quite aback by it."

"I think it's a good thing. He knows you well. He will attend to the little details of your life, so you can get on being captain without having to take the time to train a servant."

"True. But I worry that he's never been to sea. Why, my cabin on this ship is probably not the size of the butler's pantry at home."

"Oh, he's far from the first man to be plucked from the comforts of life ashore. He'll adapt, you'll see."

Mink refilled their glasses, and they sat in silence for a few minutes, watching the fire.

Finally, Walker continued, "And here is something to consider before we go on board: how are we, good friends, to act when we are captain and first? We can't pretend never to have known each other, yet we can't be as familiar as we are now. What is the middle ground?"

"Not to worry, Albert." Mink took a final sip of his drink. "I have no doubt that we will find it."

XIII

They were up early the next morning. After breakfast, Jessup engaged porters to carry their baggage to the quayside while Darling and Cannon went ahead to find boats to carry them out to the ship. Jessup and the boys rode with Walker and Mink in the first boat. Darling and Cannon followed in the second with the baggage.

As they rounded the stern of a second rate, bow oar pointed over his left shoulder with his chin at a small three-masted ship some hundred yards on. "That be her, sir. *Barbadoes* she is."

"Way enough," Walker called. The rowers rested on their oars.

"Well, Samuel, what do you think?"

The rigging on the little ship was still being set up. The fore topmast had yet to be sent up and so had about half her yards. The remaining ones floated in the water, lashed to the starboard side. But she was a handsome little ship, and it showed.

Mink tilted his head to one side, then the other. "Masts raked well aft. Fine entry, and stern tucked up a bit. Clearly American. She'll be fast. I like her."

"I, too, Samuel. I too. Let us go make our acquaintance with her. Give way."

Bow and stroke resumed rowing until they came within hailing distance where they stopped again. Bow oar stood, cupped his hands to his mouth, and called out to the ship, "*Barbadoes.*" By calling out the name of the ship, he let the men on board know that their commanding officer was approaching. Telescopes had been trained on them for a time, so this came as no surprise.

A boatswain's pipe sounded across the water as sideboys assembled at the quarterdeck, and Lieutenant Talbot took his place across from them.

The two boats pulled alongside the entry port. Bow oar hooked onto the chains as Walker stepped off onto the ladder and climbed to the deck. Mink followed and stood behind him. Talbot had done a commendable job of putting the little ship to rights, but with work ongoing on her, tools and coils of rope still lay about the deck.

As Walker returned Talbot's salute and the sound of the pipe wound down, Walker caught sight of Jessup and the boys emerging from the forward companionway. That meant that Jenkins must have gone aboard through a gun port. But how would Jessup know he could get aboard that way? And how would he know how to find the companionway? Walker put these thoughts aside and turned to the business at hand.

Talbot was addressing him. "Welcome aboard, sir. I am Charles Talbot."

Talbot was in his mid twenties, of medium height, with his uncle's round friendly face. He remained at rigid attention, clearly nervous in the presence of his new captain. It occurred to Walker that Talbot had spent his sea time so far in large ships with rigid hierarchies where the captain was approached with the utmost formality. He would have to find a way to put him at ease.

"How do you do, Mr. Talbot. May I present Lieutenant Samuel Mink."

Mink and Talbot exchanged salutes and shook hands. Talbot then introduced them to the purser, John Hayes, and the ship's clerk, Thomas Perkins. Then there was Colins' son, James, Jr., and two young midshipmen, Alexander Bird and John Wilson. The surgeon was a small slightly built and neatly dressed man named Joshua Hipple. The ship's carpenter, sailing master and his mates and a detachment of marines were expected to report in the next few days. The surveyors, Hopkins and Fletcher, were expected at any time.

As introductions were being made, Walker noticed that Jessup had taken charge of two seamen and had them using a whip off the mainyard to sway up their bags and chests from the second boat.

Walker took out his orders and turned to the business at hand, "And now, Mr. Talbot, if you will assemble the men aft?"

"Aye, sir," he said and called out, "All hands in formation aft."

The call was taken up by the boatswains, and the men hurried aft, formed by divisions. Walker stood by the binnacle and took his orders out of his uniform coat pocket. As he did, he noticed a boatswain "start" one of last men to come aft, hit him on the rear with the knot tied in the end of a short piece of rope. He abhorred the practice, and so did Darling. He would leave it to Darling to deal with.

The men formed in lines by division, shuffling silently into place, big toes carefully aligned along the deck seams. The workers from the yard looked on as Walker unfolded his orders and read them aloud to the crew. When he finished reading, he was officially the captain of one of his Majesty's ships, the closest thing to an absolute monarch that existed. He was to be obeyed without question; there was no appeal.

As the men returned to their duties, he put his orders back in his pocket and turned to Talbot. "Well then, Mr. Talbot, will you show us about the ship? I don't mean to inspect it. I simply wish to have a sense of it."

"Of course, sir," Talbot nodded.

Walker and Mink followed him as he led the way forward. They walked to the bows where one of the long nine chasers was mounted, then down the forward companionway to the gun deck where eleven nine pounders lined each side. Even with the gun ports open, it took their eyes a few seconds to adjust to the light. The tour continued down into the ship, where they had no more than a quick look at everything. Even though this was not a formal inspection, the ship looked ready for one. Talbot had done a good job of putting her to rights in a very few days. They emerged from the after companionway into the sunlight again.

"Will you join me in my cabin?" Walker said. He turned to it without waiting for an answer.

The cabin was small even for a sixth rate. None of them could stand fully upright. The accommodation, however, was vast when compared to the cramped quarters of the gun rooms Walker had occupied in previous ships. The windows that spanned the stern were open. A light breeze blew through, and sunlight sparkled off the water. The furnishings were simple.

A padded banquette seat, with storage under, ran across the aft end of the cabin under the windows. A table and six chairs served as Walker's desk and dining table. A smaller table with a chair on the starboard side would be Perkins' desk. A cot, Walker's bed, was slung from the overhead in an alcove on the port side. Jessup's sleeping space and a small pantry were just forward of that. A similar alcove on the starboard side was Walker's private head and closet.

The boys and Jessup were unpacking and stowing his things in every available space. Walker took his orders out of his coat pocket and placed them on Perkins' desk. He put the sealed orders in a drawer in the large table, sat down, and tossed his hat onto the banquette. Jessup scooped it up and hung it by the door.

"Have a seat, gentlemen, please."

Talbot sat opposite him, and Mink sat at the end.

Walker addressed Talbot, "Mr. Talbot, the ship looks to be in excellent condition, even with all the work going on. I commend you."

"Thank you, sir," Talbot replied. He sat erect, hands on his knees.

"But tell me how the ship stands in the way of men and provisions. I should like to get underway as soon as possible, but from what I saw of the men formed up, I suspect we are short of a full complement."

"Yes sir, by about twenty men. Provisions, we have a little more than half of what we'll need. I've been after the yard about it, but they have been slow to respond. I can give you a list of what's deficient."

"I would like to have that list as soon as possible. And would you and Mr. Mink also examine the gunner, boatswain and, when he arrives, the carpenter as to what they may need in the way of stores? I will take those lists to the shipyard myself. And when you see those lists, please consult each other and add what else you think will serve."

Mink and Talbot looked at each other, then to Walker, and nodded their assent.

Walker turned next to the subject of their mission. Even though he was sure that Talbot would assume that Mink had been privy to this information for some time, he spoke to them as if both were hearing it for the first time. His aim was to minimize the effect of their friendship on the good order of the ship.

"As to our mission, we are bound for the West Indies to visit certain islands of the Turks and Caicos that have yet to be carefully surveyed. The Admiralty has reason to believe that their charts are deficient in regard to those islands, if you can imagine such a thing." Walker's joke brought a laugh from Mink and a self-conscious smile from Talbot.

"There have been salt pans at work there on the large island for a long time now, but little attention has been paid to the smaller ones to the south. We are charged with assessing their strategic use by providing a better knowledge of their location, anchorages, water sources, that sort of thing. I expect our voyage to be uneventful. If all goes well, it will be a passage out, a discharge of our duties there, and a passage home."

"Will we call at Jamaica?" Talbot asked.

"Not if I can help it. That would add considerably to our voyage with no advantage to our mission, and I have no desire to expose any of us to the fever or to have us seized upon by the admiral there for other duties." This eventuality was more likely than not. Admirals on foreign stations always had a pet project or two to assign to junior frigate commanders.

"One more thing does weigh in my thoughts, however. As I am sure you have heard, a renewed war with France seems unavoidable. So, even though we are now officially at peace, we will proceed on the assumption that war has broken out and that any strange sail is an enemy. We will avoid contact where we can. With that in mind, I will want to exercise the guns as much as possible, both dumb show and live fire. To that end I will bring aboard additional powder and shot.

"There is one more thing. We are a small ship, and we will be close upon each other much of the time. I would like us to conduct ourselves with as much informality as is consistent with good discipline. Do you think that will serve?"

"I believe so," Mink said. He could see where Walker was going with this. He looked to Talbot, who was less sure.

"Informality, sir? But the men need a strong hand—-"

Walker interjected, "I was referring to the officers, Mr. Talbot. Among ourselves,"

"Oh, yes sir. Of course, sir." Talbot replied in a tone that indicated that he was not entirely comfortable with the concept.

"But now that you have mentioned the men, let me share my thoughts." Walker shifted in his chair to face Talbot. "I believe that the men want a firm hand rather than a strong one and that they are willing, even happy to work if they know what is expected of them, how they are to do it, that they are treated fairly, and that their discipline is just and consistent. Does that sound reasonable to you both?"

"It does," Mink replied.

Talbot nodded and said, "Yes sir," again appearing to be not entirely comfortable with the thought.

Walker sat forward in his chair and looked from Talbot to Mink. "Do either of you have questions of me?"

Mink shook his head. "Not I."

Talbot looked from Walker to Mink. "Nor I."

"Very good. Then we are done here. Make haste with those lists, would you?"

Jessup was just finished putting away what they had brought with them. It occurred to Walker, again, that Jessup was entirely too comfortable moving about a ship never to have been on one. He was tempted to question him about it but decided against it. Jessup had never revealed anything about his past before, and Walker could see no reason why he would suddenly reveal it now. He would keep his suspicions to himself.

Jessup took a piece of paper from a pocket and offered it to Walker. "If I may sir, you spoke of lists. These are things we still require."

He placed the paper on the table in front of Walker. Walker glanced at it. There was no need to examine it closely; Jessup would know better than he what was needed. Walker handed it back.

"Keep this with you. When I go ashore to visit the yard, come with me, and we will see to these."

"Aye, sir," Jessup said and left the cabin. It was not lost on Walker that Jessup had said "Aye, sir" and not "Yes, sir."

With Jessup out of the cabin, Walker was suddenly alone, the only man on the ship who was or could be alone. As he looked around the cabin, he spotted something familiar. There were several racks on the bulkhead by the cabin door meant to hold swords and cutlasses at the ready. Only one was occupied, by a cutlass. Walker stood, unclipped his sword from its belt and placed it in one of the racks. He took down the cutlass and examined it. It was the same that had had hung over the fireplace in the drawing room for so many years. Jessup had remembered it and brought it along. Walker hefted it, slashed left and right. It had a good feel. Replacing it in its rack, he made a mental note to have Jessup take it to the ship's armorer to have an edge put on it.

XIV

Walker spent the next day visiting the various departments at the shipyard, "encouraging" the people there to expedite the delivery of the supplies on his list. This "encouragement," in the form of payments large and small, soon bore fruit as barges began to arrive alongside the ship to offload everything from rope and sailcloth to lime juice, small beer, and, of course, rum.

On the morning of their third day aboard, Mink spotted a small boat heading their way, a solitary figure in the sternsheets. It was Holdsworth. Mink went to the cabin to tell Walker.

"Let him get aboard before we welcome him."

Once Holdsworth was aboard and his tools and seachest had been swayed up out of the boat, Mink walked out to welcome him. Holdsworth froze when he saw him.

"Good morning, Mr. Holdsworth. Welcome aboard. It's good to see you again."

Gathering himself quickly, Holdsworth saluted. "Thank you sir, and to see you as well, sir."

"Darling here will show you to your quarters and show you where to stow your tools. Please have a look at your stores and let us know what you may need in the way of supplies."

"Aye, sir, I'll have you a list today." He saluted again, picked up his seachest and followed Darling.

The last stores to arrive would be water and gunpowder. The water was delivered close to sailing so that it would remain fresh as long as possible.

74

Gunpowder was brought on board just before a ship sailed as a safety measure. If a ship's magazine were to explode in a crowded anchorage like Portsmouth, the damage would be incalculable.

Water and gunpowder were also some of the heaviest stores taken aboard. Their late delivery meant that they could be stowed in the ship in such a way as to allow a final adjustment to the ship's trim, or the way it sat in the water. A well-trimmed ship sailed faster and handled better than one that was down by the bow or stern. The man responsible for trim was the first lieutenant, and the people in charge of stowing the water and ammunition were the boatswain and the gunner. This is what found Mink, Darling, and Cannon in the jolly boat the morning the water and powder hoys were to be alongside. Darling and Cannon brought the little boat from the boat boom to the entry port and unshipped the oars as Mink stepped aboard and settled himself in the stern.

"Give way." At Mink's command, Darling, as bow oar, took a few short strokes to move the boat away from the ship and get his point, heading it in the right direction.

Satisfied, he called, "Three at the half and then full."

At this, the two men took three half strokes to get the boat moving before they put their arms and backs into full long strokes that had the boat bubbling easily through the water.

"This should do it," Mink said when they were far enough away. They backed water on starboard to swing the boat parallel to the ship so they all had a clear view of her. They had done this same thing the day they arrived on board. Darling had been supervising the stowing of provisions based on what they'd observed then. This was a final look before the water and shot arrived.

"What think ye, Mr. Mink?" This from Cannon.

Mink studied the ship for a moment or two and declared himself satisfied. "She looks fair to me." He used 'fair' in its meaning of level or proper. "And you?"

"Fair she is," Darling said.

"Fair to me," Cannon replied.

"Good then. Let's have a look at her from ahead and we're done."

Darling swung the bow to starboard. Again they took three half strokes and then stretched it out as they began moving to a point ahead of the ship.

Mink spoke. "Tell me, men. We've been aboard for a few days now. What do you think of the ship, the crew?"

Darling looked to Cannon, who glanced back over his shoulder to Darling.

Cannon spoke. "There's good and bad, like every crew."

Darling added, "There's able seamen enough and apt enough landsmen to man 'er, if 'at's what you mean."

"That's part of it, sure," Mink answered. "And what of those over you? Good lot?"

Cannon looked back at Darling before turning to Mink again.

"Aye. Talbot seems a bit unsure of 'isself but he knows his stuff. He'll work into it."

"And the midshipmen are all good sorts," Darling added. "Colins has a level head. Knows what he's about. Bird and Wilson look a bit raw, but they'll learn."

"And Holdsworth. How is he getting on?"

"Tell the truth," Darling said, "I expected he'd be upset and angry, but he's settled in like nothing happened. Quiet fellow, get's on with his mates and us just fine, like we'd never seen him at the yard."

"Course," Cannon said, "what choice did he have, eh?"

When they reached a point directly ahead of the ship, they paused again. Satisfied that she was trim, they rowed back and secured the jolly boat on deck. The poweder and shot and the water arrived that afternoon. Once they were loaded and secured, the ship was ready for sea. They would leave on the morning tide.

XV

The sky was clear. A light, steady breeze blew from the southwest. The rising sun had cleared the horizon, and the tide was about to crest. It was time to get under way.

Jessup held a plain uniform coat as Walker slid his arms into it. The sleeves and facings were unadorned. The only indication of rank was the single gold epaulette on his left shoulder. He wore plain white duck trousers and his feet were bare.

As he settled into the jacket, Mink opened the cabin door, leaned in, and said, "All's ready."

"As am I," Walker replied as he started for the door. The relationship between Mink and himself had, necessarily, become a bit formal since they had come aboard, but his suggestion that they attempt some informality had so far seemed to work.

The ship lay just above the dockyard at the edge of the fairway and just to the west of the other moored ships. There was just sufficient room to get her unmoored and onto the starboard tack. The ship's company were at their assigned stations. He could count on Darling to have experienced men in the most critical positions, but there were more than enough inexperienced landsmen aboard to make a hash of things.

Walker stood by the wheel and did a quick visual check of the ship. All appeared ready. The bars had been inserted in the windlass, and men stood by them. Darling looked back to Walker, awaiting his signal. Walker was satisfied. He nodded to Darling and called, "Windlass haul. Jibs and mizzen, foretopsail."

As the jibs and mizzen rose, the men at the foretop yard loosed the gaskets on the foretopsail, letting it fall and catch the breeze aback, holding the ship's head to the wind. The men at the windlass bars began to push, walking over the messenger line as it wound round the warping head and hauled in the much larger anchor cable. A marine drummer stood by, drumming out a cadence timed to the clicking and clacking of the pawls as they fell into the notches which kept the windlass from reversing. The windlass did not haul on the anchor cable directly; the cable was far too large in diameter for that. Instead, the messenger, an endless loop of rope, was wound round the windlass and tied to the anchor cable with short pieces of line called nippers. As a nipper neared the windlass, a ship's boy untied it and ran to the far end of the messenger to tie it to another section of the cable. As the cable was untied from the messenger, it was guided down into the cable tier where a gang of men performed the thoroughly unpleasant job of stowing the wet, noisome cable in such a way that it would pay out smoothly the next time the ship anchored.

The windlass moved easily at first, the men almost running. But as the slack began to come out of the cable, the rapid click, click, click of the pawls and the rat, tat, tat of the drummer's cadence slowed and more and more effort was required to bring the ship up over the anchor.

Finally, with the men straining against the windlass bars and cable running almost straight down into the water, a boatswain at the bows called, "Vast hauling."

The men backed off, and the pawls dropped in place to hold the windlass, and he called aft, "Up and down."

Walker took a quick look about the ship before he called back, "Break her free."

The men at the windless put their backs into it again, and the pawls clicked again with maddening slowness until the anchor broke from the mud. The windlass began to move freely, so freely that a few men fell, unable to keep their footing.

"Aweigh," Darling called aft, indicating that the anchor was free of the bottom.

Walker responded with a quick succession of orders. "Back your jibs to port. Foretopsail back to port. Let go and haul."

While the men at the windlass continued to haul the cable in, others hauled on the sheets to swing foretopsail yard to the starboard tack so that the wind would shift the ship's head to port, now that the anchor no longer held it. The courses and main topsail yard were on the starboard tack, sails still furled. If all went well, the foretopsail would cause the ship's head to fall off to port, sail would be set on the courses and main topsail, and she would be sailing on the starboard tack.

The men on the yards stood on the footropes, awaiting the order from below. The jibs were hauled aback through blocks on the starboard cathead. With the anchor free of the bottom, the ship began to turn to port. Walker watched the bowsprit describe an arc as it swung, and he waited for the right moment to shift the foretopsail and set plain sail. If he was too early, the ship would be caught all aback. If too late, she would not have enough sea room to avoid colliding with the ships anchored to port.

Walker waited. Talbot looked from him to the bowsprit and back, clenching and unclenching his right hand. Mink leaned on the lee rail, a look of relaxed, studied indifference on his face. The bowsprit continued its slow arc to port. With a last look around him, Walker gave the orders all had been waiting for. "Let go and haul the foretopsail. Shift your jibs. All plain sail."

The foretop yard swung round as the men on the other yards loosed the gaskets, and a cascade of white canvas fell, caught the wind, and was sheeted home with the mizzen. The ship moved, and Walker felt her come to life under him. It was one of the reasons he went barefoot when he could.

The ship hesitated a fraction of a second, heeled slightly to port, dipped her nose into the water a bit, rose, and began to move down the very center of the fairway. Her bowsprit pointed the way to the Channel, which could just be seen in the distance. The maneuver could not have been carried out more perfectly.

Walker turned to Talbot. "Mr. Talbot, I believe you have the watch."

"Aye, sir," Talbot replied. He saluted and turned forward. "Deck there, square things away. We don't want the fleet thinking we're a Dutchman, do we?"

The order was premature and unnecessary. The watch on deck ignored it and went on trimming the sails under the direction of the sailing master to get the ship settled on her course for the Channel. There would be time enough for squaring away when this was done.

Mink turned to Walker, smiled, nodded his head and said, "That was nicely done."

Walker smiled back. "It was. It was at that."

The wind freshened a bit as they left the dockyard behind and, still under all plain sail, made their way past the Solent and into the Channel proper. If the wind held, their course would take them across the Channel to a point where they would come about and, on the port tack, go as far as sighting the Lizard before coming about again to strike out into the Atlantic proper on a southwesterly heading.

They saw a number of fishing vessels and coastal traders as they crossed the channel, but that was all. There was, as yet, no apparent British naval presence there. Several casts of the log showed them making a little better than eight knots, a good speed for this wind. She was proving to be a fast ship.

XVI

The sailing master, Richard Stark, glanced at the chart and the traverse board. He turned to Talbot. "Any time, sir," he said.

"Very well," Talbot replied and turned to look at Walker. Walker nodded.

Mink had anticipated the exchange and had just come up the after companionway when Talbot called, "Ready about!"

The experienced hands took their stations as the boatswains pushed and shoved the landsmen to their proper places. Darling and his mates had drilled the landsmen some in which rope did what, but there was no real knowing of what you were to do in these situations until you had done it, again and again. All of this was accomplished, Walker noted, without the use of a single starter.

Going about, bringing a square rigged ship from one tack to the other involves momentarily turning her head into the wind, where there is always the chance that she will be "taken aback," meaning that the sails will catch the wind as her bow is headed into it and hold her there. This being "caught in stays" is dangerous business because the ship is not in control and the wind is pushing her back. If it is not corrected quickly, there could be damage to the rigging or, in the worst case, the ship could fall off to either side, out of control. The masts of a square-rigged ship are especially vulnerable to winds blowing from ahead because almost all the standing rigging, or the rigging supporting the masts, is set up to support them from the winds that move the ship, which are winds from aft or abeam, not from ahead.

When all was in place, Talbot called to the men at the wheel, "Alee, hard alee, put her down."

As the helmsmen swung the wheel to starboard, the ship began to come into the wind with surprising speed. Walker realized they had something to learn about how she handled.

Talbot again. "Let go and haul."

The men on the starboard sheets let them run as the men on the port side hauled in hand over hand. The yards swung round as the ship passed easily through stays to the port tack, but the foretopsail sheet nearly got away from them when a landsman lost his footing and fell, losing his grip on the sheet and knocking two other men down. Without hesitation, Colins, in charge of the foredeck crew, jumped into the man's place and helped to secure the line.

The helmsmen worked to swing the wheel back to port. Talbot looked to Stark. Stark's eyes darted from the sails above to the compass as she approached her new course. Finally, he called, "Steady as she goes."

The helmsmen steadied the wheel back as she slowed her turn and settled on her new heading, heeling slightly now to starboard. Once the ship was steady on her new course, the men at the sheets adjusted the yards so that the sails used the wind as efficiently as possible.

With the sails trimmed close to the wind, the ship picked up speed. The Barbadoes headed out of the Channel and began to feel the winds that came off the Atlantic. At the same time, she dipped her nose into larger swells that came from that same sea, throwing up an occasional fine spray over her decks. Blue water replaced green as she entered the open sea.

The course that Walker and Stark had laid out would take them to just within sight of Land's End in Cornwall where they would put the ship about on a south, southwesterly course down the Atlantic to just above the Azores. From there, they would turn west to the Caribbean to take advantage of the easterly trade winds that blew across the southern Atlantic east to west. This course was longer geographically than a course steered directly to the Caribbean, but it saved weeks of having to tack into the westerly trades that blew across the northern part of the ocean. They would take advantage of those winds to bring them home.

Jessup appeared on deck after the ship had been on her new course for some time. Walker and Mink were on the quarterdeck, anticipating the coming change of course. Mink had the watch. They watched Jessup look up at the sails, then speak to Stark at the binnacle and glance briefly at the chart before walking forward to stare out over the port bow. After a few minutes, he went below through the forward companionway, only to return and repeat this process twice more, the last time just as the Lizard at Land's End came into view. Jessup stared at it for long minutes until Mink, without waiting for a signal from Walker, called, "Ready about."

Jessup walked across the foredeck from port to starboard as the ship's bow swung to port. Walker and Mink both noticed that he stood there staring at the Lizard until it was almost out of sight.

XVII

The morning of the second day, the men began to drill at the guns. The purpose of these drills was speed, to be able to throw as much iron as possible at the enemy in the least amount of time. Accuracy was secondary. The goal was to be able to fire two to three rounds per minute. Before they could proceed to live-fire exercises, the new hands had to learn the drill of run in, load, run out, fire, run in, swab, load and run out. It was slow going at first, but repetition bore fruit as the old hands at each gun guided the new men.

After two days of this practice, Walker decided it was going well enough to reward the men with live firing. He had Holdsworth and his mates fashion a crude target out of spare planks. It was a simple raft with an upright that held a wooden "X." With the ship hove to, the target was towed out first to the port side. When the towing boat was well clear, the firing began. There were cannon balls in the ready racks next to each gun. Ship's boys known as "powder monkeys" brought flannel cartridges of black powder to each gun as they were needed. Bringing powder to the guns this way avoided the danger of explosion from too much black powder lying about the deck. When the guns were loaded, the captain of each gun poured a fine-grained black powder into the pan of the flintlock firing mechanism from a powder horn slung around his neck and, after a crude aiming with handspikes and tompion, picked up the firing lanyard and pulled.

The aftermost gun on the port side fired first, producing a satisfying roar and a great cloud of white smoke as it went off. The shot was short and wide to the left, but it elicited cheers anyway. The next gun in line fired and fell short but almost true to the target. Gun captains adjusted their aim as the port side battery fired one after another to mixed results. The aftermost gun was loaded and ready by the time the foremost gun fired.

Walker let them have three shots each before he had the target towed to the starboard side, so that battery could have a try. The whole process was repeated when the watch changed, so that all the ship's gun crews had a go at live fire. One important lesson the new hands learned from live firing, one of them quite painfully, was that a gun jumped back when it was fired, so that it was quite dangerous to stand close behind one.

XVIII

"Sail ho!"

Talbot had the watch. He called to the lookout, "Where away?"

Walker stepped on deck as the reply came down, "Port beam."

Walker slung a telescope over his shoulder and began to climb the ratlines. When he got to the maintop, aware that the men were watching him, he avoided the lubber hole and took the seaman's route, hanging upside down as the shrouds angled out under the maintop and then back in again as he climbed to the crow's nest.

"Morning, cap'n." The lookout greeted the unexpected arrival of his captain with a grin and a knuckle to the forehead.

"Good morning," Walker replied. "Is our friend still to port?"

"There, sir," the lookout said, pointing just forward of the port beam.

Walker braced himself against the circular motion of the masthead and scanned the horizon but saw nothing.

"Wait for it, sir," the lookout said. "She'll pop up."

In a few more seconds, she did "pop up" and then just as quickly disappeared. Long seconds later, she appeared again for a second or two and disappeared. The lookout had been doing his job well, Walker thought, to have spotted that sail so early.

Walker unlimbered his telescope and aimed it at the spot on the horizon where he had seen the sail. He had to let it appear a few times before he was able to focus on it. After about 15 minutes, the strange sail began to show more of her rigging. She was small, appeared to be a brig, probably a merchantman. Even if she were not, Walker had the weather gauge and would be the larger, better armed ship. Her bearing remained the same, so their courses were converging.

As Walker collapsed his telescope and got ready to descend to the deck, he asked the lookout, "What's your name, sailor?"

"McCann, sir, John McCann I am."

"Well, John McCann, you've good eyes, and you use them well. They've earned you an extra tot of rum today. I'll tell the purser to make it so."

"Thankee, sir, thankee very much." McCann grinned and knuckled his forehead as Walker began his climb down.

When he got to the deck, he ordered, "Beat to quarters but do no run out." He wanted to be prepared in case the stranger was hostile, but did not want to appear a threat if she were friendly, and a drill at quarters would be a good exercise for the crew.

As the crew set about preparing the ship, he addressed Mink and Talbot, "She appears to be a merchantman, possibly American."

To Mink, he said, "We could still use a few men. If she is American, would you like to see if there are any Englishmen aboard?"

Mink smiled, "I would, indeed."

"Very well, then. Alert the launch's crew, and take Darling and three of his men with you."

Mink saluted and went looking for Darling.

For a few years at this point, Royal Navy ships had been boarding American merchant ships and impressing seamen whom they deemed were actually British citizens. This practice would eventually lead to the War of 1812, but for now, it had occasioned no more than heated diplomatic protests, so British captains had little to dissuade them from the practice and seasoned hands to gain.

As the strange sail began to come hull up, the *Barbadoes* broke out her ensign, identifying herself as a British man-of war. The stranger confirmed Walker's suspicions by flying the stars and stripes. As the two ships came within hailing distance, Walker altered course to match the American's and, lifting a speaking trumpet to his lips, called out, "This is His Majesty's frigate *Barbadoes*. What ship is that?"

The reply, in the distinctive New England accent that had already developed, was, "Brig *Alice,* from Marseilles to Boston with general cargo."

Walker looked to Mink and nodded. Mink gave the order to get the launch in the water. The launch was clear of her chocks and moving to the side by the time Walker raised his trumpet again. "Heave to, captain. I am sending a party to board you."

There was a brief pause before the *Alice* answered, "Thank you for your offer, captain, but I am behind schedule. I cannot spare you the time just now."

"Well, well," Walker said. "Our captain has a sense of humor."

"Sense of humor?" Talbot replied, "I say insolence. Chain shot in his rigging would slow him down and bring him to his senses."

Walker glanced sideways at Talbot. "Let us see if he might be more easily persuaded."

He then spoke to Colins. "Have them open the gun ports on the port side but do not run out."

A moment after the midshipman disappeared down the after companionway, the doors on the port side gun ports swung up. A moment after that, the *Alice* loosed her sheets and hove to.

Walker turned to Talbot. "See there, we have found our man to be sensible after all, and we've saved powder and shot in the bargain."

The *Barbadoes* headed up next to the *Alice* as the launch touched the water. Her crew dropped aboard, followed by Darling, two of his mates, and Mink. In the matter of a few minutes, the launch was alongside the merchantman with tossed oars and Mink was climbing the side to confront a less than welcoming captain and his crew. Darling and his two mates followed close behind. Several of the crew of the launch, armed, came aboard and formed a line along the rail by the entryway.

"Lieutenant Samuel Mink of His Majesty's navy," Mink said as he approached the captain.

"Ezra Clark," the captain of the *Alice* responded, staring directly at Mink.

"Well then, Captain Clark, will you please ask your men to assemble here with us? And may I see your muster."

Clark turned to his first mate, "Johnathan, all hands, with their protections," as he turned to his cabin to retrieve the list of his crew.

"Aye, sir," the mate responded, and called for all hands on deck. The men began to shuffle reluctantly into a rough formation, each one holding an official looking document, their "protection." These were issued by inspectors of customs or notaries in seaports in the United States and by American consuls in foreign ports. The document identified the holder by age, height, hair and eye color, and any prominent scars or tattoos. It certified that the he was an American citizen, and therefore not subject to impressment in a foreign navy.

By the time the men had formed up, the captain was back with a journal. He opened it to a page that listed the crew signed on for this voyage. Mink counted the number of men on the journal and the number of men on the deck.

"By my count, captain, we are one man short. Is everyone on deck?"

The captain at first appeared surprised, but he collected himself and looked over the assembled men and the men still tending the ship.

Clark hesitated, "Ah, yes," he said, as if remembering. "I had forgotten Sexton. I should have noted him as 'run.' He did not report aboard before we left Marseilles." A man who had run was a deserter, a man who had "jumped ship" at a port.

Mink looked from the captain to Darling and nodded. Darling and one of his mates headed for the companionway. At first, the captain made a move to stop them, but he thought better of it.

"You'll not find him there," he said.

"Then there is nothing to concern you, is there?" Mink replied. He and the other of Darling's mates started going from man to man, examining their protections.

It was not unheard of for someone to procure more than one protection by securing one in one port, a second in another port, a third in a third, and selling them because, at this time, there was no central registry monitoring them. Protections could be sold from one man to another because the descriptions on them varied from very specific, including such things as scars and tattoos, to little more than age, weight, height and hair color. Mink was handed one of the latter. It stated that the man was born and raised in Philadelphia.

Mink questioned the man, "You're from Philadelphia, I see."

"Yes, sir," he replied.

"Lovely city. Beautiful view of the ocean in the morning from Castle Island, isn't it?"

"Aye, sir, beautiful view."

"Well," Mink said, looking down at the protection, "Mr. Thomas, if that is your name, it's unfortunate for you that Castle Island is in Boston Harbor, and the ocean cannot be seen from Philadelphia. Step out and go collect your things."

"But, but I--" the man said. He looked to captain Clark who just looked away. Finding no help there, he went below to get his kit.

Just as Mink finished examining the last man, a seaman carrying his chest came up the companionway, followed by Darling, his mate, and the man Mink had sent below.

"We found your Sexton, Mr. Mink," Darling said cheerfully. "'E were curled up in an empty barrel."

"Good work, William, good work. Get these men in the launch, then. We're almost done here."

Before he turned to leave, Mink said to the men still assembled. "Which of you will now join us of own his free will? We are bound to the near West Indies to do some surveying and then back to Portsmouth where we expect to pay off. No stop at Jamaica, so no fevers. Good pay, good food, and a reasonable man for a captain. What say you? Who will take the King's shilling?" Mink was referring to the traditional one shilling bonus men were paid when they enlisted. He waited a moment.

When there was no reaction, he said, "Ah, well," and turned toward the entry port.

As he did, he heard, "I'll join. I'll take the shilling."

Darling's head popped back up in the entry port as Mink stopped and turned to see a slender young man with blond hair step forward. As he did, he looked to Captain Clark. Their eyes met for a moment.

Clark turned to Mink as if to say something, thought better of it and turned back to the sailor. "This isn't the end of it for you, Foster, not if I have any say in it." No one moved until the captain added, "Well, go on then. Get your chest and get off my ship. Good riddance for now."

The man went below and was back in minutes, carrying his sea chest and a small canvas shoulder bag. He saluted captain Clark with a smile as he left the ship.

XIX

Walker had just emerged from his cabin wearing a broad-brimmed straw hat Jessup had packed for him. As his eyes were adjusting to the bright tropical sun, the call came from the lookout. "Land Ho! Two points off the starboard bow."

Mink had the watch. He turned to Walker, grinned, and spread his arms, palms out, as if to say, 'See? I told you so.' He had predicted they would make landfall before noon. It was about half eleven.

Talbot appeared in the after companionway as Walker spoke to Mink. "Indeed, it appears you have done it. We shall go and see. Bring us starboard a point, will you?"

Mink relayed the change of course to the men at the wheel while Walker slung a telescope over his shoulder and climbed the main shrouds to the crow's nest, again avoiding the lubber hole on his way over the maintop.

"Welcome, sir." The lookout greeted him with a smile and a knuckle to his forehead before pointing over the starboard bow. A tiny spot of green could just be seen bobbing up over the blue of the water, the wisp of a cloud hanging over it.

"Good morning, McCann. You've done good work once again."

"Thankee, sir, thankee," McCann replied with a smile as he moved to port to make room for Walker.

Walker opened the telescope and braced himself against the mast while the ship settled on her new course. Fifteen miles was about as far as one could see from the masthead of the *Barbadoes* so, at their current speed, they would be at the island in a little less than two hours.

Walker stayed aloft until he could see the shape of the island. The Admiralty chart showed no topography, just a narrow, north-south strip of land. The island that revealed itself to Walker was grass-covered and low-lying from its southern end to about two thirds the way north. There, it rose up to a form a modest hill covered in brush and the occasional clump of trees. Beyond the hill, it gradually became low-lying again for the rest of its length. Surf broke against most of it, and there was little to nothing to see in the way of beaches. The prevailing winds were from the east, so they would anchor on the west side of the island where the water would be calmer and where Walker hoped they would find a suitable landing place.

Their course took them just south of the island. They hove to the south and west of it where Walker climbed as far as the maintop. The view from there revealed the west side of the long southern third of the island to be a sandy beach that sloped gently into the sea. It appeared a perfect landing place, but they had to know the depth of the water before they could get any closer. Walker sent Colins, Darling, and two of his mates in the jolly boat to take soundings and sample the bottom. They came back to report that there was ample depth of water from about one hundred to one hundred fifty yards out, but beyond that it dropped off quickly. The sounding lead came back up with its tallow coated with sand, which confirmed what they could see through the crystal clear water: a good holding ground. Towing the jolly boat behind, the ship made its way to a spot halfway along the beach and about a hundred yards out.

There was more to anchoring a square-rigged ship than finding a good spot and dropping the anchor. Once a ship was at the place where the anchor was to be let go, the ship was turned into the wind and, under reduced sail, allowed to be intentionally taken aback. The wind pressing back against the sails stopped the ship and gave her sternway to pull on the anchor line and set the anchor in the ground. A ship did not need all of her sails set to accomplish this maneuver, so most of them were furled before she got to the anchoring point. The *Barbadoes* was under foretopsail, jib, and mizzen, and she was moving slowly on the starboard tack as as she approached her intended anchorage.

Walker had the deck. "Head her up. Square the foretopsail."

The men at the wheel turned it to starboard as the hands at the braces brought the foretopsail yard square across the hull. With her head to the wind, the ship slowed to a stop and began to move astern. Both anchors were lashed to the catheads, timbers that jutted out from the hull at the bows. A soon as she stopped moving forward, a crewman with a hand axe chopped through the rope lashings and the starbord anchor splashed into the water, dragging the heavy anchor cable with it. Walker let her move astern until a sufficient length of anchor cable had paid out to permit the anchor to dig in securely.

"Secure the cable! Brail up! Strike jibs and mizzen."

The cable taughtened and then slacked off as the ship came to rest, and the sails were gathered to the yards.

X X

By the time the ship was secured and the men had had their dinner, it was too late to begin a formal survey of the island, but Hopkins wanted to go ashore to "get a sense of the place" before he began work the next day. Walker and Mink decided to tag along, if for no other reason than to feel solid ground underfoot. Darling took the little party, that included Hopkin's assistant and Adam and Andrew, over to the island in the launch. With Walker's approval, Jessup had suggested the boys assist Hopkins. It would expose them to a valuable skill, and Jessup could easily fill what time it took from their duties serving Walker.

They landed near the southern end of the island. As Walker stepped out of the boat and took a few steps up the beach, he experienced that odd feeling of "sea-legs," where the land sways under you for a bit while you adapt from rolling deck to solid land.

They began to walk north along the beach. Darling went with them, leaving the launch's crew with instructions to pick them up at the north end of the island. A gentle breeze blew from their right as small waves rolled onto the sand at their left. The sun hung a few diameters above the western horizon. Walker and Mink were barefoot. They walked in silence for a while, a silence broken only by the occasional comments between Hopkins and Fletcher. The boys ran back and forth from the water to the sand, delighting in the sun, sand and crystal-clear water they could never have hoped to image only weeks before.

After they passed a few pieces of driftwood that looked similar, Walker stopped and picked one up.

"What do you make of this, Samuel, and you, Darling?" he said as held it up for them. "We've passed several like this."

It was a small piece of what appeared to be oak planking, shattered into jagged pieces and painted black on one side.

"It looks like a splinter from the strike of a cannonball," Mink said.

"Aye, that it does, Mr. Mink. And it's got a bit o' grass on it, so it's nothing as happened recent," Darling added.

He was right. There was a deal of green growth attached to all of the pieces, so whatever had happened had happened some time back.

Walker tossed it into the water. "But some ship took a beating," he said.

They continued to walk along the hot sand until the beach gave way to a slight, rocky hill covered with low grasses and the occasional bush or two. The rough ground had Walker and Mink regretting their decision to go barefoot while Darling, his feet rough and calloused from years on decks without shoes, barely noticed. They paused at the top to catch their breath, telling Hopkins to go on, that they'd catch up.

Mink turned and sat on a small outcropping of rock. Walker sat next to him. Darling continued to stand. Mink waved him to sit. He picked a sandy spot of ground in front of them. The launch had gone on ahead and was beached at the top of the island. Most of the crew were stretched out on the beach. One man was actually swimming, a skill most sailors, surprisingly, never learned.

Mink spoke to Darling, "Tell us, William, what do make of the ship now that we've been at it for a while? Good crew?"

"Aye, Mr. Talbot knows his business. Midshipmen are good sorts. Do your job's all they ask."

"And the men?"

Darling considered the question for a moment, shrugged, and said, "Good and bad, like all ships. Most are good men, willing to do the work. A few have to be reminded now and then, if you know what I mean. Oh, and we have a sea-lawyer, that fellow as volunteered off the American. Foster it is."

"But there's one on every ship, isn't there?" Mink asked. "If it wasn't him, it would be another."

Sea-lawyers were sailors who questioned authority with spurious claims that certain orders didn't have to be followed because they were illegal for one reason or another. They were generally harmless, if annoying, cranks.

"But 'is one's a bit different. 'E and a few of 'is mates'll go off and talk among themselves, lookin' over their shoulders like. Makes me uneasy."

"There's always one, as you say." Walker said, "But there's a fine line between sea-lawyering and mutiny. See if you can find out what they're talking about, will you?"

"I'll do what I can, sir, sure. But, that aside, what I've seen and heard on the passage over is that we have a generally happy ship."

"Aye, that," Mink added. "But what of Holdsworth, William? I was expecting him to be quite put off by being aboard, but he seems to be getting on well."

"'E is. But 'e seems 'e's developed an eye over his shoulder at times, on edge 'e is some. Good worker though, knows his business."

Hopkins and his party had reached the top of the island and were standing by the launch. The sun was nearing the horizon and would soon, as it did in the tropics, disappear quickly.

"Time to get on," Walker said. He stood and began to walk toward the launch.

It was just dark when they got back to the ship. Light from the open gunports and the ship's lanterns danced across the water as Darling laid the launch against the entryport. They were back just before the call of "Down hammocks" sent the men to retrieve their hammocks from the nettings and get them slung before the 8 p.m. call of "Ship's company lights and fires out" would see the common areas of the ship go dark. Commissioned and warrant officers in the wardroom and gun room would not have to douse lights until 10 p.m.

X X I

The morning found Hopkins, Fletcher and the boys setting up Hopkins' equipment on the southern tip of the island to begin the formal survey. Mink was with them, tasked with getting an accurate noon sight so the island could be placed more precisely on subsequent admiralty charts. He was also curious to see "how the mathematics of this surveying business worked."

The men in the launch returned to the ship and joined in the daily routine. Awnings had been rigged over the length of the ship to keep the sun off, both to spare the crew the worst of the heat and to protect the ship itself. Direct sunlight in the tropics dried out and shrank deck planking and softened the tar that sealed the decks. Some of the crew were hosing the deck down with seawater and scrubbing it clean with brushes. That scrubbing removed most of the dirt, but the really thorough cleaning was done with holystones, twice each week for the main deck, usually on Thursdays and Sundays, and once per week for the lower decks. A holystone was a piece of stone about the size of a pillow, flat one one side and round on the other, that had a ring bolt fixed to it. Two lengths of rope were secured to the ringbolt. The deck was wetted and sand was spread over it before two men dragged the stone back and forth over the wet sand. Holystoning was, of course, hard on the wood and wore it away much as sandpaper would, so admiralty regulations specified that it be done only to the extent necessary to keep the decks clean. Other members of the crew polished the brass with brick dust. The launch's crew joined the men in the other boats who were scrubbing the ship's sides.

Walker spent part of the morning going over the ship's accounts with his clerk, Perkins, and the ship's purser, Hayes. The purser was personally responsible for all the stores aboard, and he charged the crew for everything from tobacco and candles to the food they ate. There was ample opportunity for abuse in this system, but Hayes' accounts appeared to be in good order. Walker made a mental note to have Mink take a look at them now and again. He spent the rest of the morning with his rough log and the master's log, writing up a fair copy for the Admiralty. He was just finishing at about one o'clock when Mink returned from the island.

"So how goes it on the island?" Walker asked as Mink entered the cabin. Walker had just eaten and Jessup was about to clear the table. Walker pointed to a chair. "Sit. Would you have something to eat."

Mink took a chair across from Walker. "Thank you, but we took lunch with us. A glass of wine would serve, though," he said as he reached for the decanter, and Jessup brought a glass. "Hopkins is about half done. He's measuring off points and distances on a sketch his assistant's made. They'll draw up a fair copy later," he said as he poured himself some wine. "And my sight showed the Admiralty chart was off by only about half a mile."

"So we accomplished that at least, and we'll bring back a fair charting and description of the island they didn't have before. And tell me what you think of surveying now that you've seen it."

"Well the mathematics is quite simple, for me at least, a bit of angles and trigonometry and such, and far too much, I think, of dragging chains and tapes about to measure distance. Andrew and Arthur are having fun with it, though." He took a sip of wine. "But I did get to examine his instrument, his theodolite. It measures angles both horizontal and vertical with great accuracy. Oh, and I found more debris."

"More splinters?"

"Splinters and a bread barge."

"A bread barge?" Walker looked surprised. "So all this came from an English ship, and a warship at that."

A bread barge was a large wooden tray that sailors used to bring the allotted amount of bread, a hard biscuit called hardtack, to the members of their mess, or the men they ate with, at mealtime. The bread barge was unique to the British Navy.

"So it appears. I wonder that there is so little debris if the ship wrecked here."

"Perhaps it wrecked here. Or perhaps there was simply an engagement with another ship, and what is here are just the splinters shed in that engagement."

"Yes, but the bread barge? How was that shed in battle?"

"She may have gone to quarters during a meal. No one would have thought to secure a bread barge in that circumstance."

"Sensible, yes. But we shall probably never know."

"No. Curious though."

They sat in silence for a moment or two. Jessup had cleared the table and refilled the decanter.

"So, have you decided where we go from here? And when? Hopkins should be done by tomorrow morning, latest."

"If he is, we can probably get underway tomorrow. Let's have a look at the chart."

Walker took a rolled up chart from an overhead rack and spread it out on the table.

"There are these two islands here," he said, pointing to a spot about twenty miles to the west and a bit north. "They appear to be relatively well charted, so we should need do no more than fix their position, confirm their shape is correct, and look about for water and such. They are large enough that there should be streams there."

"And after that?"

"After that I propose to sail west to something less than seventy-two degrees before dropping south some five miles or more and turning east again. This should reveal any islands in that area that are not charted and will take us back close to the position you sussed from Jenkins' numbers. That will let us 'fall upon' whatever we find at the spot. I don't want to seem to be heading to that spot. Let me get that paper."

Walker took the key from around his neck and opened one of the drawers in the table. The paper was in the back of it. He brought it out, and Mink picked up a parallel rule, measuring off the position as Walker read the latutide and longitude of 71 deg. 40" 3' W, 21 deg. 13" 0' N to him. Mink touched the spot with his finger. It was about five miles south of the two large islands they would explore next.

"Very good, then," Mink said, and he drained his glass. "Let me go communicate this to Mr. Stark so he can prepare."

"Go. I shall be up presently," Walker replied.

XXII

He was on deck when the launch came alongside, bringing Hopkins and his party back to the ship. The boys were first to scramble aboard. They had yet to learn that the most senior in a boat was the last to embark and the first to disembark. Hopkins' equipment came next, the theodolite, tripod, a folding table and instrument cases. All were handed up with extreme care. The launch's crew had put Hopkins' mind at rest a bit by securing a line around the theodolite case and sending the line aboard first to be tended by crewmen as the case was carried up the side.

When all was aboard, Hopkins turned to Walker. "After I have all this put away, I should like to show you our work so far, if you would see it?"

"I will be happy to see it," Walker replied. "Take your time and bring it to my cabin when you have all this secured."

Hopkins nodded to Walker and turned to the business at hand.

Mink and Talbot followed Hopkins into the cabin some fifteen minutes later. Hopkins carried a large, rolled-up sheet of paper that he spread out on the table to reveal a rough but accurate sketch of the island overlaid with his calculations.

"Before we start," Walker said, "would anyone care for a glass of wine?" He ignored Mink and, when Hopkns and Talbot politely declined, he said to Hopkins, "Please begin, then."

Hopkins pointed to a spot on the north end of the island and began. "We started here, at the north end where Lieutenant Mink would take his sight at noon. You can see his latitude and longitude written in there. I drove a stake in there and we then proceeded to drive stakes and measure point to point down the west side of the island, measuring the angles stake to stake carefully to permit us to accurately portray the shape of the island and orient it on a larger chart. Fletcher has made a number of drawings of details that will be added to the larger chart."

Lines on the map were drawn from the point of origin in the north down the west side of the island, connecting points where stakes had been driven. The angles between the lines had been measured and noted at each point. Positions had been staked and lines drawn about half way up the east side of the island.

"Tomorrow we should need no more than two or three hours to complete our measurements of the east side. We will then have an accurate measure of the position and orientation of the island, and a good depiction of what is sand, rock, foliage, and such, but only that. As I understood my instructions from the Admiralty, what is desired includes position, shape and description, but not a thorough measurement as would be required in setting boundaries for such things as the passing of title. Am I correct?"

"Yes," Walker replied. "This is quite enough for our use in navigation and an immense improvement on what we have now. Let me show you." Walker took down the chart of the area he and Mink had looked at earlier. "See here," he said, pointing to what appeared to be no more than a small spit of sand on the existing chart.

"What the current charts show is featureless, probably less than half the size you have measured, about a mile too far east and a bit south, and thus quite useless for navigation. So, for our purposes, yours is excellent work."

"Thank you, sir," Hopkins said with a nod and a smile.

"And while we have this out," Walker continued, "why don't we look upon what we will do for the remainder of our time, shall we?"

Hopkins and Talbot leaned over the chart as Walker described the route he and Mink had laid out earlier. The two islands to the west showed more detail on the chart than the current one, so they all thought that the charted location and description might be relatively accurate. If this were the case, Hopkins estimated that it would take two days or so at each one to verify their shapes and features and to fix their positions.

Walker wanted to weigh anchor as early as possible the next day, so Hopkins and his party were on their way to the island as soon as the crew stood down from breakfast. As they worked, Darling and the launch's crew stood off the beach and made additional soundings to determine the extent of the holding ground there. The surveying party was back alongside a little after noon. All that remained was to hoist in the launch and secure it. As it settled into its cradle, Talbot, who had the watch, turned to Walker. Walker nodded.

Talbot called forward, "Windlass haul!" and the process was underway.

The ship was headed into a gentle east wind, but her course was west by northwest. Walker and Mink watched from the quarterdeck as Talbot took charge of the complicated business of getting the anchor up and turning the ship one hundred and eighty degrees. The commands came steadily, one after the other. Foretopsail mizzen and jib were set. Foretopsail back, then as the anchor broke the ground, foretopsail braced to starboard to swing the bows to port. Let go and haul to swing the foretopsail to port as the bows came around, ship on the starboard tack now. She heels slightly to starboard as the forecourse, maincourse and all topsails are set, then comes to an even keel as she begins to run before the wind. With the ship closing on her new course, the topgallants drop into view, and all sails are sheeted home.

XXIII

Their course to the next island, Big Ambergris Cay, passed some five miles north of the latitude and longitude Mink had identified, close enough that anything there should be visible from the crow's nest. When they were close enough, Mink slung a telescope over his shoulder and joined the lookout. At first he saw nothing, just an expanse of open sea. He took the telescope from his eye, waited, and looked again several more times.

Nothing. Perhaps, he thought, they would find something there when they passed closer on their way back from the west. He took a look further to the west. Did a spot of green appear and vanish as quickly? He kept staring at the place he thought he had seen it. Did he see it again? Or had he simply wanted to see something too badly? He took the telescope from his eye and waited a few minutes. Took another look.

There it was. The green appeared in the telescope and stayed there, hovering in the heat just above the blue of the water. He stared at it for a long few minutes before he collapsed the telescope and climbed down.

Walker was waiting for him when he stepped onto the deck. "The smile on your face gives the game away. So there is something there?"

"Indeed there is," Mink replied as they walked to the cabin. "Green as Ireland shining in the sun. But it is west of the spot I sussed from the numbers."

"Let us leave it there for now," Walker answered as they went past the sentry and ducked their heads to enter his cabin. "I don't want to seem too eager by deviating from our plan."

They got to the first island late that afternoon and dropped anchor at a point south and just west of it because a shallow bank appeared to run well south of it. Walker sent the men to dinner. They would begin work the next day.

The following morning, Hopkins, Fletcher, and the boys left the ship early to start the survey of the island up the west side. Walker, Mink, Darlng, and Cannon followed them in the jolly boat later in the day, rowing up the east side. They planned to meet at the top in time for Mink to take a noon fix.

They pulled in to the beach about three quarters of a mile up to look at a small stream that emptied there. As they walked along the beach, they came across more of the splintered oak planking. Darling showed it to Cannon, who had not seen the pieces from the previous island. He agreed it looked like the splinters cannonballs made when they struck a ship. A little further up the beach, they found something else: the cover of a gunport. One hinge had been torn off and the other was bent, as if a giant hand had pulled it up and off the hull. A portion of the rope hauled on to open it still clung to it, frayed and grown over with sea grass. When they turned it over, they saw that it was partially blackened on the inside.

"What are we to make of this?" Walker asked.

They all stood in silence for a moment until Cannon observed, "I can see the other stuff as pieces torn up by cannonballs in a fight, but no cannonball'l tear a door off. Splinter it, sure, be it open or closed. But not take it off like this."

"Aye," Darling replied. "But what if it were no cannonball? Suppose two ships come together, one to board the other, say? Rubbin' together like that could tear a door off."

"It could. Well taken," Mink said. "Albert?"

"That makes sense, surely. Either way, there was an engagement here of some type. Let's walk on."

They walked a little further up the beach before they returned to the boat. They stopped a few more times on their way to meet Hopkins, finding another stream but nothing more. The two boats rowed back together and were at the ship in time for dinner.

Hopkins finished his work on Big Ambergris Cay on the morning of the third day and moved on to Little Ambergris. He was done there late in the afternoon two days after that. They would wait for the morning to make sail.

Mink dined with Walker that night. After he cleared the table, Jessup brought out a pot of coffee and two cups. He again put a small bottle of brandy on the table by Mink.

"You'll spoil him, Jessup," Walker said.

"I have heard it said that you cannot spoil a good man, sir," Jessup replied, echoing what Mink had said of Darling and Cannon back at the house.

"Well said," Walker replied. "Well said," as Mink laughed out loud.

They sat in silence for a moment or two before Walker said, "Well, here we are, well along our 'survey,' and no sign of gold or any misdeeds by Jenkins. What do you think of that?"

"I'm disappointed, of course," Mink replied. "But I'm still convinced that those numbers of his were meant to be a simple cypher to disguise latitude and longitude."

"I agree that makes sense, but you saw nothing there, just the island to the east of it. And what of the other number?"

"I honestly have no idea. I thought it might make some sense when we got here, but I'm afraid it's come up as meaningless as the others. I don't want to go back to old Burns empty-handed, but it looks like that's what's to happen."

"Oh, I wouldn't worry about that," Walker replied. "This voyage was his idea. We didn't press it on him. They want to know about the gold, and I'm sure your idea was as good as any they've come across--maybe the only idea they've come across. Remember what Burns said, he wasn't so sure we would find anything, but they were willing to give it a go. They'll get to correct their charts and that was their stated purpose, so that should be enough to justify the business and satisfy Burns and whoever else is behind this."

"I imagine. But wouldn't it be grand to come sailing back up the channel with chests of gold? And wouldn't it be even better if a prize court determined it to be property captured and recaptured, and we were to have a share?" Mink said with a big smile.

"Indeed it would. But that regulation applies to ships captured and recapturerd. It would make an interesting argument, but I'm not so sure a prize court would be easily convinced."

XXIV

They got underway the following morning and sailed south and west, coming upon a chain of small islands that did not appear on the Admiralty charts. They did no more than visit them briefly to estimate their size and shape, take soundings and note their position. This done, they sailed west to seventy two degrees before turning south and then east again to set a course that would take them back to the island Mink had sighted. Their plan was to approach it from the south, sail round it to the latitude and longitude they had sussed from Jenkins' numbers, and come to anchor to the west of it.

They had passed to the south of the island and come about onto the starboard tack. They were just a bit to the west of it when the cry came from the lookout, "Deck there! Look below! Starboard side!"

Walker and Mink went to the rail, leaned over, and peered into the crystal clear water. On the bottom, there was the outline of a ship. They were just beginning to pass by it. The water blurred many of the details, but it was a ship, lying partly on its side, looking, as Mink later said "broken." The presence of gunports, just visible at that depth, indicated a warship.

Walker and Mink stood looking, peering down as the watch on deck ran to the rails and men came up from below to see what the commotion was. Holdsworth went to the rail, looked over, then looked back to the quarterdeck. His eyes met Walker's briefly before he walked slowly to the forward companionway and disappeared below.

As the wreck passed astern, Walker called down to the helm. "Mr. Stark! Bring us about and pass over this spot again. Slower this time, if you can."

"Aye, sir," Stark replied. He too had been at the rail. He gave the orders that would turn the ship and set her on a reciprocal course, then reduced sail to take way off. The Barbadoes moved slowly as she passed over the wreck again. Most of the crew were on deck and lining the rails, looking down in silence.

As the wreck passed astern for the second time, Darling, who had been peering over the rail himself, took charge. "That's enough now. Back to your work. There's no more to see here." The men dispersed, talking quietly among themselves.

Mink spoke, still staring into the water. "It appears we have found the sources of our splinters."

"Aye," was all that Walker could answer.

They went back to the business of getting the ship around the island and anchored.

X X V

"Join me in my cabin," Walker said to Mink as the anchor dug into the ground.

Walker hung his straw hat on its peg next to the door and sat on the banquette, looking out on the water. Mink turned a chair from the table and sat. Neither spoke as Jessup brought a mug of lime juice and water for Walker. The ship was enjoying the luxury of fresh water that had been taken on at Big Ambergris Cay. He set a glass of wine by Mink and left the decanter as he went on deck.

Mink took a sip of wine. "So, have we found the *Diligence*?"

Walker stared into his mug. "I believe we have, and there is one more person on board who knows that it has been found," he replied as he looked up at Mink and took a swig of juice.

"So it's time to speak with Holdsworth?"

"Don't you agree? We have that scrap of wood from his shop and now, it appears, from the very ship itself. There is no chance now for him to cling to the story about the Frenchman and the storm. I say it's time to confront him."

"And I. Let me go find him."

Mink walked to the door and went outside. As he stepped past the marine sentry into the sunlight, he came face to face with Holdsworth.

"Was ye coming for me, sir?" Holdsworth asked.

Taken aback, Mink hesitated a moment before saying, "Aye," and standing aside to let Holdsworth enter the cabin. Holdsworth walked in, took off his hat, and looked directly at Walker.

"I had naught' to do wi' that, naught."

"The ship? The *Diligence*?" Walker replied.

"Aye. I had naught to do wi' it. It was all Jenkins, him and the others. You see--"

Walker held up a hand to stop him. "Sit down," he said, indicating a chair at the table that faced the stern windows. Holdsworth sat stiffly erect, holding his hat in his lap as Walker and Mink took chairs on the opposite side of the table. The afternoon sun was at their back, casting them partly in shadow and illuminating Holdsworth.

Holdsworth stared down at the table as Walker began to question him.

"So the ship we passed over is the *Diligence*?"

"Aye, but I had naught to do wi' what happened to her, and I knew naught of the gold either, at first, anyway."

Mink's and Walker's eyes met. Here was confirmation that Jenkins had the gold aboard.

"Go on," Walker said. "Tell us first what you know about the gold."

"Precious little, sirs. It must 'ave come on board the week before we sailed for England. There was one or two nights that 'e, that Jenkins--'im and a couple of the others went ashore late. With 'im reducin' the lookouts to one man, and that man one of 'is lickboots. Someone was cheek enuf t' ask what it was all about, and 'e told it was all Admiralty business and none of theirs, if they knew what was good for 'em."

"Who were the men with him? The 'lickboots', as you say."

"'Is bosun an' some of 'is mates." Holdsworth recited some names. They were all from the list Burns had given them.

"And then he came here?"

"Not directly, 'e didn't. I'm no master's mate, but it seemed we sailed a bit into the Atlantic before turnin' back 'ere. There was talk and argument between 'im and the others up to that. You could 'ear 'em but not all what was said. It was about the gold, though, 'at you could tell. At's when he asked me to make the boxes."

"Make the boxes?" Mink asked.

"Aye, boxes like the gold was in. 'E showed me one o' them as he 'ad and 'ad me fix up t'ree more. Said it was Admralty business and to keep it mum. While I done that 'e put about and came to t'ese islands, pretty much as you 'ave, stoppin' at one after t'other."

"But not the main islands north of where we have been, the larger ones?" Mink asked.

"Just where we been, far's I remember."

"Go on," Walker said.

"Well, they was back and forth in t' boats at each island, at night, mostly. The crew was wonderin' more and more what they was up to. I don't know that 'is first even knew, just that it was 'Admiralty business' as Jenkins said. But some wasn't believin' it by then. There was talk 'e was off on a frolic of 'is own an' not for the admirals. It all ended, though, when we got to 'ere."

"To this island?" Walker asked.

"Aye, 'ere. 'E anchored where you saw her. After lights out they was off in a boat again. Same thing a second night. Mornin' after that they was getting ready to leave again, and Jenkins, 'e says to me, 'ere, you get in.' So I does, and we go to the far side of the island."

"Why you, if you weren't privy to what they were up to?"

"I dunno. But 'e was someone I come to know startin' far back. We served together, off and on. Knew each other."

"Go on."

"We rows back to the island, beaches th' boat and, as we're gettin' out..." He stopped and looked down, took a deep breath, and looked back at them. "Ats when it 'appened. We was all stunned by the noise." He hesitated again, "Then the smoke and the flames. We just froze like and stared at it. I seen pieces of the ship come splashin' down about 'er as she sank, puttin' the fire out on the hull while little pieces 'at floated about it burned and went out."

He stared at his hands. They sat in silence. Mink started to reach for his glass and stopped. Holdsworth took another deep breath and continued.

"Eventually, we rows back to where she were. T'ere was only bodies, bodies and pieces like you see after a battle. And pieces of t'e ship, spars and splinters. Not'ing we could do, so we rows back to the island and sits on the beach. I dunno why or for how long. But we sat t'ere for a long time before Jenkins up and says, 'It was an accident. But we can't tell 'em that, can we? Too many questions, eh?' Or some such like that. They all agrees with it right off, so I keeps my mouth shut and goes along, not bein' part of 'em an' all. Then he tells us the story of the Frenchy and the storm an' the rest of it. Says when we get through it all, we can come back an' split it all up, cut the admirals out."

"What did he mean by that? 'Cut the admirals out'?" Mink asked.

"I dunno, but the others all seems to and nods ok, so I nods w' 'em. 'E then tells the story again we all told to th' court, and we rehearses it back to Jamaica."

"And the court accepted it, and the Admiralty, too, until Jenkins was found under the pier. Tell us about that," Walker prodded.

Holdsworth squirmed in his chair a bit, trying to get comfortable. Mink got a second glass, poured wine in it from the decanter and held it out to Holdsworth.

He hesitated.

"Take it." Walker said.

Holdsworth drank and continued. "When we starts workin' at Wool'ich, I asks him about goin' back for the gold, and 'e says wait for peace as it were too dangerous then. After the peace, it's wait til 'e finds a way to go back. Others ask 'im, and soon there's no answers. Then one of 'em dies in an 'accident,' or so it seems. Then another. Soon it's down to me, and I see it's 'im or me."

"Why didn't you go to the authorities and turn him in?" Walker asked.

"What? Go up and say, "Ere gents, I stole your gold, blew up your ship, lied about it all, and could you please stop th' bloke 'ere from killin' me now?'" He looked from Walker to Mink with a shrug of his shoulders.

"Go on," Walker said, conceding the obvious.

"So I'd long seen it were no accident, the ship goin' up as it did, and I knew I'd never see no gold, not knowin' where th' island is, and the only way I'm safe from Jenkins is if he's gone, once and for all. I'm also thinkin' a simple killin's too good fer 'im, after what he done to the ship and 'is men and all. That was why th' cage." He took another swig of wine, looked from Walker to Mink and added, "What's to become of me, now, sirs?"

"Tell me first, why did you come to us? Why not stay quiet?"

He took another drink of wine. Mink refilled his glass as Holdsworth continued. "I been carryin' this wi' me for a long time now. It only gets 'eavier. It were time to put it down." He sipped again and continued, "I knew ye were on to me at Wool'ich. I seen yer man take the chip."

"From behind the workbench?" Mink asked.

"Aye. And when I come on board and seen you, and wi' us sailin' for th' West Indies, I knew it were no survey mission. I knew ye'd figured there were no Frenchy and no storm. When ye found the ship, I were done."

He stopped and looked from Walker to Mink, asking again, "So, what's to become of me?"

Walker took a sip of lime juice and answered, "I don't know. That's not for us to say." He looked at Mink and continued, "If what you say is true, you had no hand in the theft of the gold or the loss of the ship. Your sins, as it were, are lying to the court and assaulting an officer. There is little excuse for the lie, and I cannot say what a court might think of the assault if it believed, as you did, that you were in mortal danger from Jenkins. Your prospects are not the best but, I think, better than you see them. The fact that you came forward speaks in your favor." He turned to Mink, "Samuel?"

"I agree. And in coming forward you have aided us in this. That counts for you, as well."

"Do this," Walker said, "Go back to your duties for now. Should anyone ask what you were doing with us here, say I asked you here to discuss the condition of the ship. That should serve. She has just had an ocean crossing after a refit. Such a request by a captain of his carpenter should not seem out of place."

Holdsworth slouched against the back of his chair, took a deep breath, and exhaled. "Aye, sir. I will that."

"And if you think of more that might be useful, let us know."

Holdsworth stood. "I will, sirs, I will. And thank ye. Thank ye both." He turned to the door and stopped. "There was one odd t'ing Jenkins said in th' boat once. One of 'em asked 'im how could 'e find it again, the gold, and 'e said something about numbers, 'avin' all th' right numbers. The man asked what 'e meant by it, and all 'e said was 'e knew what 'e meant and that was enough, almost like he found 'e'd said too much."

He looked from Walker to Mink again, put a knuckle to his forehead, and went out into the sunlight.

Walker drained his mug as Mink refilled his glass. They sat in silence for a few moments. Walker spoke first.

"Do you think he was being truthful?"

"I do," Mink replied, I have no doubt that that was the *Diligence*, and why would he make up a story about gold?"

"And what about what he says was his part in it? He tries to come off the innocent."

"Aye, but now it's his word against Jenkins'. I'd give him the benefit of his words. You know as well as I that there's little chance that the Admiralty would charge Holdsworth. Right now, they have a tidy story of a valiant encounter at sea and an heroic small boat passage by the survivors. Will they retract that for the truth of the murder of a ship's crew?"

"No. You are right, of course," Walker said. "So, now we know what happened to the *Diligence*."

"And we know Jenkins made off with some of the gold."

"All we have to do now is to find it." Walker said. "Even if it's here, that still leaves us, by what I could make of this island, with about ten acres or so to dig up."

"Do not despair just yet. Only about half of that looks to be sand or soil that can be dug into, and we still have the second set of numbers. Let us see if they mean anything, now that we have an island to apply them to."

XXVI

They anchored just before dinner. Hopkins thought it would take a day and more to complete his work there, so they decided to wait for the morning to begin.

Walker and Mink, Darling and Cannon went over to the island with the survey party after breakfast the next day. The island was just like the others they had visited, rock, coral and sand covered in brush and grasses. They again wore straw hats and long sleeved shirts against the sun, but by now Walker and Mink had adopted the wearing of shoes against the rock and coral. Darling had a small shovel to dig with; Cannon carried an iron bar.

Hopkins, Fletcher and the boys began their work on the western tip of the island. Walker and the rest went to the center of the island where the sand and soil were. Their plan was to spread out and walk the area, looking for anything that might indicate that the ground had been disturbed--a depression in the soil or a mounding, anything that might look out of place. They started walking side by side, about ten paces apart, making several sweeps across the area. They stopped several times and dug down five feet or so only to find rock or to have water begin to well up in the hole.

When Hopkins returned to the ship, he brought Fletcher's sketch, with his survey lines and notes for Walker to look at, as had become his custom. The sketch was on the table when Mink came in to have after dinner coffee with Walker that night. Mink picked it up and glanced at it. It showed the island with lines drawn on it to indicate where Hopkins had made his various measurements. Overlaying all those was a triangle drawn from corner to corner of the three corners of the essentially triangular island with the values of the angles noted. He was about to roll it up when he stopped, stared at it, put it slowly down on the table, and turned excitedly to Walker.

"Albert. Albert. Come here. Tell me what you see."

He stood back and pointed at the sketch. Walker stepped over to the table and looked at it.

"What of it?" he asked.

"Look carefully. Look for numbers."

Walked stared at the sketch again. "I'm afraid you have me. There are quite a few numbers."

"The angles, Albert, the angles defining the island," Mink replied.

Walker looked again and said, "You show me."

Exasperated, Mink pointed to the three angles of the large triangle. "Here, see how Hopkins has drawn a triangle to measure out our island?"

"Yes, I see that."

"And now look at the values of the angles he has measured."

Walker read them off. "89, 47, and 44."

"Now read the numbers from Jenkins' paper."

Walker retrieved it from the drawer and read, "884844." He still looked puzzled.

Mink began as if instructing a child. "What is the sum of 89, 47, and 44? Take your time and write it out, if you must."

Walker studied the numbers for a moment, picked up a pencil and wrote them down. "180," he said.

"Correct!" Mink said. "And what is true of the angles that make up a triangle?"

Walker stared blankly at Mink.

Mink spoke slowly. "Do they not teach the mathematics at Eton?" He again spoke slowly. "The sum of the angles in a triangle is 180. Now, look at Jenkins' second number."

Walker stared at it a moment and turned back to Mink with a delighted smile of discovery. "It's not one number. It is three."

"Yes, yes," Mink said delightedly, "Go on, you're getting it."

"And they add up to 180," Walker said, surprising even himself.

"Precisely," Mink said. "They don't exactly describe Hopkins' triangle, but there is no real functional difference."

"But what do they signify?"

"I don't know," Mink replied. "But they were obviously very important to Jenkins, and I believe they will lead us to the gold."

They both stared at the sketch and the angles for a few minutes until Mink gestured to a rack of navigational instruments on the buklkhead next to Walker. "Here," he said. "Hand me that protractor and the parallel rules, won't you?"

Walker handed them to him. Mink placed the protractor on the westernmost angle and laid the rule over it, dividing the angle in two. He them drew a short line along the rule in the middle of the island. This done, he did the same thing with the northern angle. When he was finished, there was an "X" just to the east of center on the island.

When he was done, he stepped back and grandly waved a hand. "There," he said. "What do you think of that?"

"I think you may have solved the riddle. Good work, Samuel."

Mink smiled and took a bow.

"But, Samuel," Walker asked. "How could Jenkins have plotted that out without instruments such as Hopkins'?"

Mink put one hand on his hip and grasped his chin with the other as he stared at the sketch for a minute.

"Good question," he replied. "I think he might have done it with no more than a boat compass and a straightedge, such as these parallels."

The compass Mink referred to was a small one, mounted in a box that was customarily carried in a ship's boat such as the launch. It could easily be removed.

"It would be as simple as this," he continued, and he placed the parallel rule along the side of the triangle that ran from the west to the north. "Place the compass here, lay the rule over it, and sight to a pole held at the north end of the line. The pole can simply be an oar held upright. Then mark the degrees the rule passes over on the compass, sight to an upright at the easten end, and mark the degrees shown. To get the angle, deduct the lower number from the higher, and your heading to the point you want to identify is halfway between the two degrees you sight. Now do the same from the north point, and you have the second line of your 'X'. The third line's just for safety."

"That would work, surely," Walker said. "But if this is what he did, how can we know we are putting our compass at the same spot he did?"

"We can't, but even with some error in that, we would be narrowing the area we had to search to something quite manageable. And the fact that Hopkins' angles and Jenkins' are almost the same leads me to believe that, if we use Hopkins' stake marks, we will be very close when we mark our 'X' on the island."

"Good," Walker declared. "Then let us go back and see if we can do this by ourselves. I'd rather not involve Hopkins and the rest unless we have to. Although we should involve Talbot. I'd rather have him know what we are up to rather than have him think we are running behind his back."

The sun was on the way down by this time, so they would wait for morning to go back and see what might be at their 'X'.

XXVII

The next morning, Mink located the stake Hopkins had set at the western end of the island and set a box compass there that Darling had taken from the launch. He sent Darling and Cannon to the northern and eastern markers with oars to use as range poles. Walker and Talbot dragged two more oars to the center of the island. Mink placed a parallel rule on top of the compass and sighted from the stake, first to one pole and then the other, noting the bearings to each. He then sighted from the stake along the bearing half way between those two, waving to Talbot, who held one oar upright, to move the oar until it intersected that bearing. Talbot then laid the oar on the ground along the line of the bearing.

Mink moved the compass to the northern stake, and they repeated the process with Cannon and Darling at the western and eastern stakes, with Talbot laying the second oar down where the two lines crossed. They then watched as he dragged the first oar on top of the second to form an 'X'.

The 'X' was on an uremarkable piece of ground. Nothing about it showed that it might have been disturbed in any way. Cannon picked up the shovel and began to dig. He got down less than three feet before the shovel hit something solid with a dull thunk. He removed a few more shovelfuls to reveal an oak board.

Mink looked to Walker. "That's it! We've done it," he crowed.

"We shall see," Walker answered. Everyone gathered closer as the men began widening the hole. The sandy soil yielded quickly to reveal the tops of three oaken boxes of about the size Holdsworth had described.

"Haul them up here and let's see what we have," Walker said. "Pull one of the boards off one."

They pulled the three boxes up out of the hole by the rope handles built into the ends of each and lined them up. Darling stuck a shovel between two of the boards and pried one off.

The men peered into the box, silent.

"Rocks," Walker finally said. He pried up boards on the other two. "More rocks. We have found boxes of rocks."

They stood and stared at the crates.

Mink put a hand on his waist and stroked his chin for a minute. "Aye, we did that, but is that all we found?" He turned to Cannon. "Dig some more."

Cannon got back in the hole and began to throw up more shovels of the loose, sandy soil. It was getting wetter now as he went deeper and water began to seep in. Less than two feet further down, the shovel hit something with that same dull thunk they had heard earlier. Cannon looked up and smiled. Darling grabbed another shovel and the two men widened the hole to reveal three more crates sitting there. They brought all three up and pried a board loose on each to reveal closely packed gold bars.

"That's more like it," Mink said. "That's what the other boxes were for; they were decoys, meant to have us think we'd got the wrong spot, to turn us away."

"That was good thinking on your part, Samuel. Should we credit those pirates and smugglers from whom you claim to descend for that?"

"I see no reason not to. I'll claim my lineage gladly," Mink replied with a smile. "But let's get these boards back in place and get these crates aboard. Do we want the decoys for any reason?"

"Not that I can think of," Walker replied. He turned to Cannon and Darling, who were hammering the boards back over the gold with rocks. "Go on and rebury them when you're done there."

Talbot had been silent for some time. As the two men placed the decoys in the hole and filled it, he asked, "What are we to tell those on board? Surely it won't go unnoticed that we are carrying three heavy chests back with us."

"You are quite right," Walker said. "There will no doubt be speculation, but those few who do ask can be told--" He stopped and turned to Mink. "What do you say we tell them it's Admiralty business?"

Mink smiled. "Admiralty business, it is. Make it so."

Walker turned back to Talbot. "I think Samuel has it. If anyone has the temerity to ask, Charles, tell them it's Admiralty business." To Darling and Cannon, he said, "Did you hear that?"

Cannon turned to him with a look of studied innocence on his face. "Chests, sir? Why, we doesn't know of any chests." He and Darling looked at each other, shrugged, picked up the first of the chests and headed to the beach.

They took the chests to Walker's cabin and lashed them to ringbolts on the deck that had once secured a cannon. The arrival of the chests did not go unnoticed, but no one seemed to pay any particular attention. One of the people who noticed and did pay attention was Foster. He stood and watched and then went below.

X X V I I I

The next morning, they weighed anchor and sailed south and then west as far as they had sailed two days earlier, when they had documented the chain of small cays they had found prior to discovering Bush Cay. Then it was south and east again, to enter the Atlantic and turn north and east for home.

As they began sailing west again, the sky to the southwest darkened at the horizon, and the barometer showed a prounounced drop in air pressure. The wind that had been blowing from the west shifted to the southwest. Walker and Stark feared a storm coming on and ordered the topgallants taken in and the courses and topsails reefed. The glass stayed low for the rest of the day, and the darkness at the horizon grew briefly before subsiding again.

By evening, the glass had risen and the threat of a storm seemed to have passed them by. As the wind shifted to the west again, they set the topgallants and shook out the reefs. Stark, who had some experience in these waters, cautioned Walker that large storms such as this one appeared to be could move unpredictably. They would watch the glass carefully.

By the next morning, they were working their way out into the Atlantic, heading north and east to pick up the westerly trades that would take them back to England.

The wind began to blow from the west as they approached thirty degrees north, signaling that they had found the westerlies, but these were neither strong nor steady, prompting Stark to warn again of the possibility of heavy weather. It was a full week after they encountered the westerlies that the winds began to settle in and blow with any force and regularity. They had covered little distance in that time, even though Mink and Darling had overhauled the sail locker in search of studding sails, staysails and any other bits of canvas that might catch just a bit more of the wind and make up for the lost time.

As they gained northing and the westerlies picked up strength, they brought the extra canvas in piece by piece, but the little ship still showed a satisfying turn of speed. Everyone on board now looked forward to a fast passage home.

XXIX

Walker was at his desk the next morning when the call came down from the lookout, "Sail ho! Starboard quarter!"

He rose and made for the door. Talbot had the watch, and he stood by the rail on the quarterdeck, peering off to starboard. He called to Walker as Mink appeared in the after companionway. "Nothing to see from the deck, sir."

Walker took a a telescope from the binnacle, slung it over his shoulder, and climbed to the crow's nest. McCann greeted him with his big grin and a knuckle to his forehead.

"Mornin' cap'n."

"Good morning, McCann. So, I have your sharp eyes to thank once again, eh?"

"Oh. I just 'appened to chance upon 'er, sir. Over t'ere she'll be," he said, pointing off the starboard quarter, "'bout t'ree points, a bit less."

Walker braced himself against the gentle roll of the ship and focused the telescope on the area McCann pointed to. On the horizon, he could just see the royals of a ship that looked to be on a course to cross their track aft of them, heading south and west while they were on a course north by east. McCann brought his telescope to his eye, and the two men watched the sails slowly slip from view.

Just as they did, McCann asked, "Were she turnin', sir?"

Walker was wondering the same thing. Was the distance between those masts shortening as she slipped below the horizon? Had she seen the *Barbadoes* and decided to give chase?

"I don't know, McCann, but I, too, wonder."

Both men kept their glasses to their eyes for long minutes more, but all traces of the ship had disappeared.

Walker collapsed his telescope and turned to McCann. "I guess we'll know soon enough if he's after us, eh?"

"Aye, sir, soon enough, if 'e 'as the legs to catch us," McCann grinned.

"Aye, that," Walker replied with a smile and a nod as he swung a leg over the side of the crow's nest and began his descent.

Mink and Talbot were waiting for him when he got back to the deck. He spoke to them as he walked to the binnacle to replace the telescope. "It is a ship, and from all appearances, a large one. I do not know but that it has seen us and chosen to give chase. Let us assume it has."

The warrant officers and midshipmen gathered round as he continued. "Samuel, you and Darling crack on a bit more sail. Don't overbear her, but I think we'd all be more comfortable with another knot or so."

Addressing everyone, he went on, "When we left England, a renewed war with France was spoken of as a certainty. The question was when, not if, it would begin. For now, we will assume that war has broken out again and act accordingly. I will not beat to quarters yet, but be prepared for that, should that ship reappear."

Addressing the officers, he said, "I shall be in my cabin if you need me."

Back in his cabin, Walker retrieved his orders from a drawer in his desk and reread a provision from the order that he had been instructed to open only when at sea.

> Should you succeed in accomplishing this secondary mission, you are requested and required, once you have accomplished your primary mission, to return to England with all dispatch. You will avoid, where at all possible, contact with other vessels, friend or foe, and you will engage any other vessel only to defend yours.

A captain was supposed to be eager to confront the enemy and engage in combat. To be seen to turn away or to run was a sign of weakness, punishable by death. This order clearly contradicted traditional rules, giving him clear authority to crack on and avoid the stranger. It was, Walker also realized, a less than subtle mandate from their Lordships to protect the gold and to get it to them "with all dispatch."

X X X

By the time Walker came out on deck again later in the afternoon, Darling and his mates had rigged topmast studding sails, and the ship had picked up a knot or two. There was still no sight of the stranger. The sky to the southwest darkened again as the afternoon wore on and the wind picked up a bit. Stark's pessimism about the weather continued even as they sailed into clear weather ahead of them.

The men were sent to dinner, and the watch changed. The ship's routine carried on as the sun began its slow descent behind them. Walker invited Mink and Talbot to dine with him, and Jessup had just served coffee and was returning with Mink's brandy when the call came again, "Sail ho!, dead astern."

"That answers your question as to whether he was turning," Mink said.

"Indeed it does," Walker answered as he headed for the door. "Why don't you find a telescope and join me?"

As Mink got up to follow him, Walker stopped in the door and turned to Talbot. "It will get crowded if all of us try to get aloft, Charles. Why don't you stay and enjoy the coffee while it's hot?"

To which Mink added, "And try a bit of brandy with it. It's good for the soul and improves upon the taste."

Talbot saluted them with his coffee cup as Walker took a telescope from the rack by the door and slung it over his shoulder. Mink took one from the binnacle and made for the port shrouds while Walker began his climb on the starboard side. Mink unashamedly went through the lubbers hole, whereas Walker once again studiously avoided it.

As Mink and Walker crowded into the crow's nest, the lookout moved forward of the mast to give them room, pointing dead aft. "She'll be there, sirs. Pops up and down. Give it a wait, and you'll see 'er."

They unlimbered their glasses, focused on the horizon, and gave it "a wait." McCann's relief was no less eagle-eyed than McCann. The ship did indeed pop up and down, showing precious little of itself but for the very top of it's main topgallant. They watched as the stranger appeared briefly and then disappeared again.

Mink spoke first. "There's no question he's gaining on us, but it's slow going for him. Last we saw of him was over eight hours ago. I won't bore you with the mathematics, but I can't see him gaining much more on us by dark. Little at all, if we mount some more studding sails."

"Very well, make haste with it then."

"Directly," Mink said as he swung a leg over the side of the crow's nest. As he began his descent, Walker turned to the lookout. "What's your name, sailor?"

"Allen, sir. William Allen the second. There's two of us, you see." It was common, when two men on the same ship had the same name, to refer them as the first and the second.

"Well, William Allen the second," Walker replied, "your keen eyes have earned you an extra tot of rum. I shall speak to the purser."

"Thankee, sir, thankee very much." William Allen the second replied with a wide, somewhat toothless grin and a knuckle to his forehead.

Mink started calling orders to Darling while he was still descending the ratlines. Talbot was waiting for them on deck. As they headed to the sail locker to rouse out more sails, Mink explained what they had seen and had decided to do. At the same time, Holdsworth and two of his mates began to sort out spars from the spares stored on deck, searching for some suitable to carry the additional sails.

Studding sails, or stunsails, were carried on a spar slung from the ends of yardarms. They projected out from the yards as far as possible and gave the impression that the ship had sprouted wings. Getting them in place involved a good bit of marlinspike seamanship in the tying of complex knots, both to secure the sails to the spars and to mount the pulleys, called blocks on a ship, so that they could be hoisted into place and adjusted from the deck.

The first to go up were on the main yard, where Mink and Darling had experimented with them earlier. Then, on the main topsail yard. Stunsails were generally carried only in light winds, so they held off setting more, particularly because Stark was not still not at all convinced that they had outrun the bad weather that had crept up out of the southwest twice now. Even so, casts of the log before and after the addition of the stunsails showed them picking up about a knot.

When the sails were set and drawing well, Walker and the two lieutenents returned to the cabin. The sun, still about a diameter above the horizon, had begun to cast a bronze glow on the wake that flowed behind the ship under the open stern windows.

Jessup set out brandy and rewarmed coffee as they again took their seats at the table. While Mink applied himself to the brandy, Walker took a sip of coffee and leaned back in his chair.

"Setting more sail is all well and good," he said, "but I think it might also be prudent to begin lightening the ship. What say you to disposing of some of the additional round shot we took on?"

"Certainly that before guns or water," Mink replied.

"Shall I see to that?" Talbot asked.

"Pass the word for Cannon, and task him with it."

Talbot opened the door and spoke to the marine sentry who stood outside it. "Pass the word for the gunner."

The marine stamped one boot smartly on the deck as marines were wont to do when responding to orders and cried out, "Ship's gunner to the cabin! Ship's gunner! Pass the word." His voice was loud enough that it made passing the word quite unnecessary.

As Talbot took his seat again, he asked, "How much of the round shot, exactly?"

Walker replied, "I purchased an additional ten for each gun. The yard allotted us 55 rounds per gun, so we had 65 total for each. I believe we expended about 5 per gun in live fire exercise, so that leaves us with 60 to a gun. Let us initially dispose of the additional 10 purchased for each and make it 250 shot. That should leave us about a ton lighter."

The sentry opened the door and Cannon stepped inside as Walker finished speaking.

Cannon looked to Walker. "You sent for me, sir?"

Talbot replied, "I did, Cannon. We're about lightening the ship. Will you see to disposing overboard of 250 round shot?"

"250, sir? Overboard, sir? Aye, sir."

"And you'll mind the trim?" Mink added.

"Course, sir. We'll take from the rows starting in the middle, work fore and aft. And begging pardon, sir, but we'll not engage the stranger, then?"

Walker replied, "Not unless we must. Our orders are quite specific that we are to return to England with all dispatch, and that is what we are about."

"Course, sir. No disrespect, sir, but the men are curious, and some think we're running from a fight."

Mink and Talbot looked to Walker. "None taken, Cannon, and thank you for that," Walker replied. "And now make haste with that shot."

"Aye, sir. Haste it is," he said as he headed for the door.

Walker took a sip of coffee and looked at Mink. "It looks as if it's time I speak to the men. I want to put an end to that business about running from a fight." He swallowed the rest of his coffee and walked to the door, took his hat off the rack, and walked onto the deck to the sound of the marine sentry stomping to attention. Mink and Talbot followed him out. Darling stood with Stark in front of the mainmast, looking up at the set of additional sails as the light of day began to fade with the setting of the sun.

Walker called to Darling. "Darling, all hands aft in formation, if you will."

"Aye, sir, aft in formation," he replied as his mates took up the cry and it began to echo below decks.

Quickly, and without a starter in sight, the men gathered aft and formed by division, toeing the lines of the deck seams.

Walker climbed to the quaterdeck. Mink, Talbot and the midshipmen stood with their divisions.

When they were assembled and quiet, Walker began. "We have completed our mission, and we are under orders to return to England with the utmost dispatch. We are ordered to avoid contact with other vessels, friend or foe, if at all possible. That is why we are doing what we can to outdistance the ship that is following us, not out of any fear of the ship itself. We are a ship with a mission, not a patrolling frigate spoiling for a fight. But, if the stranger should overtake us, we will fight him, and we will fight to win. Until then, we will do our duty, follow orders, and make haste for England."

Walker paused. The looks on the faces of the assembled men told him nothing. He looked to Mink and nodded. Mink gave the order to dismiss. The men broke ranks and started back to their duties about the ship, talking quietly among themselves.

Walker turned, walked to the taffrail, and stood watching the ship's wake. The upper limb of the setting sun slipped below the horizon as Mink joined him.

"Do you think the stranger's still with us?" Mink asked.

"I have little doubt. And, apparently, Cannon has little himself. See, he has brought up chain shot."

The long-nine stern chaser was mounted on the quarterdeck. As Walker spoke, he pointed to the chain shot that had replaced the round shot in the rack next to it under the taffrail. Chain shot were two nine-pound balls joined with a chain. When these were fired, the balls would spin with the chain stretched between them, aiming for a ship's rigging to disable it.

"Good for him," Mink replied. "Though I don't know how effective it might be if our pursuer is of any size."

They stood quietly for a minute, watching the wake until Mink suddenly burst out laughing. Walker turned to him.

Mink stopped laughing and put a hand on Walker's shoulder. "I'm laughing because it just occurred to me that we are living Jenkins' fiction. Don't you see it? Here we are, straight from the pages of the court martial, being chased by a superior force while a storm threatens."

It was Walker's turn to laugh.

XXXI

Walker was up before the sun the next morning. Coffee in hand, he left his cabin and greeted Colins, who had the watch.

"Good morning, Colins."

"Morning sir," Colins saluted.

"All quiet?"

"Aye, sir," Colins replied. "Wind's freshened a bit is all. Given us a knot, maybe."

Walker glanced up at the sails. Everything was drawing well. There was no need to make any changes for the present. After a quick glance at the traverse board, he turned toward the quarterdeck. "Carry on, then."

He climbed the ladder to the quarterdeck and stood alone by the taffrail, looking aft, watching the ship's wake unspool behind it into the darkness. The ocean's swells had increased overnight, driven by the storm that continued to stalk them. Walker felt those swells as the deck rose and fell under his bare feet. He took a sip of coffee and turned to look forward. Dawn glimmered dimly to the east, several points off the starboard bow. Within the hour, there would be enough light to reveal whether they had lost the stranger.

Mink appeared on deck, coffee in hand. He spoke briefly to Colins, glanced at the traverse board, and climbed to the quarterdeck.

"You're up and about early," he greeted Walker.

"Aye, as are you," Walker answered with a smile.

Mink took a sip of his coffee. It smelled warmly of brandy.

"So, do you think your little adjustment has allowed us to slip away?"

Once night had fallen, Walker had ordered a change of course slightly to the north and west of the original, hoping that, by dawn, they would be well out of sight of the stranger.

"We shall know soon enough. Although I would be surprised if he hadn't been expecting us to try something on him."

Mink turned and looked forward, "Soon enough, indeed. Here is the sun."

Mink's sun was no more than a faint glow on the horizon, but it meant that morning had come and that they would quickly know if they were alone.

Mink started for the ladder. "Duty calls. I have the next watch."

Walker returned to his cabin for a breakfast of cold meats and hardtack. The call came as he took his last swallow of coffee. "Sail ho! Off th' starboard quarter!"

He left his hat on its hook and grabbed his telescope from its rack. The sun had climbed above the horizon, and the wind had freshened a bit. As Walker climbed the ratlines, he could feel the shrouds adjusting to the increased pressure.

William Allen the second was in the crow's nest. "Mornin', sir," he greeted Walker as he indicated a spot just a point or to to starboard from dead astern.

"Good morning, Willaim Allen the second," Walker said, scanning the sea where Allen pointed.

The wind was still picking up, and it took him a few moments to sort the tip of the other ship's mainmast out from the whitecaps now rolling off the waves that followed them. He unlimbered the telescope, leaned back against the mast, and studied the other ship for long minutes. The stranger had found them and was gaining on them, slowly, but gaining still. He closed the telescope and prepared to go over the side. As he did, William Allen the second looked at him with an expectant grin.

Walker smiled, "Aye, an extra tot it is."

Mink, Talbot, the midshipmen, and the warrants were waiting for him when he got back to the deck.

"I've no doubt," he told them. "It's our friend. I can only assume that he's seen us, and he appears to be gaining."

He spoke to Mink, "What say you we crack on more sail? We've still room for more stunsails."

Mink turned to Darling, but he and Holdsworth were already on their way to rouse out more spars and canvas.

Stark, ever the conservative, spoke up. "Wind's freshened and she'll continue to rise. No offense, sir, but look astern. That darkness bodes no good. If we put up more sail, we'll lose it, sure."

Stark was right. Bad weather was moving over the western horizon.

"No doubt," Walker answered. "But for now, I should not mind sacrificing a bit of canvas, even a spar or two, in pursuit of speed."

The few extra stunsails gave her a little boost in speed, but not enough, Walker feared, to let her outrun her pursuer. It was time to lighten the ship again. The fastest way to do this would be to dispose of several cannon, but Walker feared the effect it would have on the men, especially since he had told them they would fight if they had to. Getting rid of water was the only alternative. They had left England with more than enough water to make the passage to the Caribbean and had filled the casks before setting out for England again. On top of that, their return was near a straight line helped on by the westerly trades, a shorter route than the westward crossing that had seen them sail well south before heading west. They had water to spare, so water it was.

Mink was overseeing the lashing down of the remaining spare spars. Walker motioned to him and met him by the binnacle.

"It's time to lighten her again, Samuel," he began, "and I'd rather lose some water than cannon. Do you argee?"

"I do," Mink answered.

"Good, then. I'll leave it to your discretion as to how much, but there should be a goodly surplus."

"Aye, that. There's plenty enough to spare and to make a difference in speed."

He turned and called to Darling. "Man the pumps and come with me with two men. We're sending some water over the side to lighten her again."

Several men unlimbered the handles of the pumps as Mink, Darling, and two of his mates went down the after companionway. Mink quickly did the math about how much water they could spare and pointed out to

Darling the casks to be emptied, keeping in mind the trim of the ship. As Darling's mates started the casks, the water flowed to the bilge and from there was pumped up and over the side.

The next cast of the log showed a small increase in speed. Mink joined Walker the next time he climbed to the crow's nest. The stranger had gained a bit on them in spite of Walker's efforts. The white of his topgallants now showed steadily above the horizon, where before they had dipped down below it and risen again. They were easier to see now, as the color of the sky had turned leaden under the advancing storm.

Walker took his telescope from his eye. "Well, Samuel, what think you? How soon before he's in range?"

"At this rate, not today. Perhaps he'll lose interest overnight, or that storm will get serious and give us both more important things to think about."

"If he hasn't lost interest by now, I doubt he will overnight," Walker replied, "especially since he's gaining on us. I know I wouldn't were it I. It appears we will deal either with him or the storm."

They were up to the crow's nest a few more times that day. And, while they could not be sure, it seemed that they had matched the stranger's speed and that, while he was still in sight, he was no longer gaining.

XXXII

Walker turned in early that night but dozed off and on more than he slept. He lay in the dark, staring at the repeater compass over his head as eight bells sounded. In yet another attempt to lose his pursuer, he had ordered another small change in course after night fell. The wind had increased, and the little ship spoke to him about it, her timbers creaking as she moved over steadily mounting swells, so he was not surprised when Mink opened the door to his cabin.

"Wind's up, Albert," he said. "We may want to get some sail off her."

"Samuel, I've been expecting you." Walker was fully dressed but for a coat. He swung his bare feet onto the deck and stood as Jessup appeared with a simple jacket and helped him on with it.

The wind was on their port quarter and, with all he canvas she had set, was putting a heavy strain on the rigging. Stark stood by the helm, which he had double-manned, his expression at once worried and accusatory. Did the man never sleep, Walker wondered of him. Colins, who had just relieved Mink, and Darling stood next to Stark.

"What say we strike what you put up yesterday, and see if that eases things sufficiently?" Mink said.

Walker moved forward, looking up at the sails. They were carrying a lot of canvas for the wind, but the strain did not appear to be anything she could not handle. He decided against it at least until dawn.

He turned to Mink, "Not just yet. She's riding well. Let's wait til dawn and see where our friend might be."

Darling had anticipated an order to strike sail and had his mates at the ready. They dispersed quietly after Walker spoke. As they walked away, Stark spoke up. "Begging your pardon, captain, and meaning no disrespect, but we'll have to get some sail off, and soon. The wind's shifted to the north some, and that storm's closing us sure and fast."

"Indeed, Mr. Stark," Walker replied, shouting over the wind. "But give us 'til dawn, will you, 'til we know if our friend's still about?"

Stark nodded reluctantly, saluted and turned his attention back to the ship.

Walker called to Mink. "Join me for an early breakfast? I believe I smell Jessup's coffee from here. And bring Talbot with you if he's up."

"With pleasure," Mink called back.

Mink found Talbot and returned to the cabin where Jessup had laid out a breakfast of hardtack, cheese, some very good strawberry jam preserves, and a pot of his excellent coffee to wash it down.

They ate in silence for a few minutes. Mink, tapping a piece of hardtack to encourage the weevils to move out, began the conversation. "I fear Stark's right. Wind's not going to let up."

"I've no doubt that he is right," Walker answered, "and I'll be happy to bring in sail if we have made any strides on the stranger."

"And if we have not?"

"Then I will leave it up. As I said, better to lose canvas than speed, eh?"

"Aye that," Mink replied.

Again, they ate in silence. Talbot made a few mostly unsuccessful attempts to soften the hardtack with jam while Mink made his breakfast of cheese and coffee. It was not yet dawn, but dawn's light was making itself known. The sky outside had lightened perceptively, but it was still darkly overcast. Talbot looked from Mink to Walker and went back to urging weevils from his hardtack.

When he looked up at them again, Mink asked, "What's on your mind, Charles? I sense that there's something."

Talbot looked down at his hardtack, then back at Mink and Walker. "Well, I'm thinking that this fellow must be at least a fifth rate, probably bigger. He carries twelve-pounders anyway, probably eighteens. How do we fight that? It's not that I don't care for a fight, mind you, I just don't see how we match him."

It occurred to Walker that Talbot had probably never seen action. It was a fair question.

Mink spoke first. "Nelson probably summed it up when he said, 'Never mind maneuvres, always go at them.'"

"Excellent advice," Walker added, "to a point. But one should have some idea of what the enemy is and what one will do when they do get to them."

"But would we really just go at this fellow?" Talbot asked. "Mismatched as we are?"

"That would not be my first choice," Walker replied. "But there is something to be said for the element of surprise. He cannot be thinking we will attack him, so, if the opportunity presents, it is a valid tactic."

"And it would not," Mink added, "be the first time a smaller ship has taken one larger. There is much to be said for the fighting spirit."

"Indeed, but let us not get ahead of ourselves, here," Walker continued. "Our first plan is to outrun this fellow. If we cannot, then it will be a duel of our stern chaser against his bow chasers with chain shot, trying to take down rigging."

Mink leaned into the conversation. "And a lucky shot by either side could end the business right there." He turned his attention to Talbot, "Speaking of lucky shots, have I ever told you of the time…"

Mink launched into a story that Walker had heard many times before, so he let his mind wander, only to have it pricked by the thorn of self-doubt. Being a master and commander had been a relatively easy undertaking up until now, he thought. But getting a ship from one place to another was not really a difficult task. The real test of his abilities would occur when they came to grips with the stranger. Was he up to the challenge? It was one thing to be a lieutenant and follow orders in battle. He had done that many times and had no doubts about his ability. But what would he do when the fate of his men and the ship was in his hands, when he was the one who issued the orders? Was he up to it?

"Sail ho!"

The cry snapped Walker from his musings and stopped Mink in the mid-sentence. The sun was just above the horizon. The sky had brightened perceptively but so gradually that they had not noticed. Walker took his telescope from its rack and started for the ratlines on the mainmast in the blustering wind.

Stark, who was leaning over the starboard side looking aft, stopped him. "No need for that, sir. I can see his royals from here."

The stranger had gained on them overnight. Stark, Mink, and Talbot followed Walker up the ladder to the quarterdeck. Stark was right. There was no need for a telescope. The top of the stranger's royals were clearly visible.

"It's the storm, sir," Stark said. "That weather's come to him first, pushing him up to us. He's feeling it more than we."

Indeed, the wind had increased, and the rising sun showed the sky to the south and west to be darker than it had been the day before.

"Even at that," Mink said, "she must be carrying a wonderful amount of sail to have made up that much on us. But we're still out of range."

"Aye," Walker replied, "but that's no reason to be complacent. Clear for action."

Mink called the order down to Darling, who passed it on. Gun crews manned their guns. Ship's boys strewed sand on the deck to give the men at the guns better traction, and all loose gear was secured or stowed below. Cannon and two of his mates hurried by him with powder charges for the stern chaser, carefully sewn flannel bags filled with black powder. Walker watched as Cannon filled the pan of the flintlock mechanism with a finely ground black powder from the powderhorn slung over his shoulder, cocked the mechanism, stood back, and yanked the firing cord. A satisfying red flash and a puff of white smoke told him it was working properly. He and the gun's crew ran the gun inboard and loaded a canister of powder and a round of chain shot. Cannon filled the flintlock pan with fine powder again, and they ran the gun back out.

Stark returned to his station by the wheel. Walker noted that, for once, Stark had said nothing about reducing sail. Even so, Walker now wondered how long they could carry all the sail that they did. The wind whipped at his hair and blew the windward lapel of his jacket over his chest. The waves had increased considerably, as well. They had a following sea and were being driven onto the backs of significantly larger waves than they had been the day before. The little ship's fine entry forward tended to ease the motion and took some of the pressure off the rigging, but the shrouds still complained of the strain they were under.

Walker remained on the quarterdeck, watching as the stranger's royals came into full view, and then his topgallant yards. As they did, he heard the muffled roar of a cannon. The stranger had fired her bowchaser. The whitecaps made it almost impossible to see where the shot fell, or even if it had come anywhere close.

Mink was at his side. "I make us still a bit out of range. I think he's doing no more than announcing his presence."

"I agree," Walker replied. "But we'll be in range soon enough. Hoist the colors."

Mink passed the order, and the signal midshipman and two men appeared and ran the ensign aloft. Cannon stood by the stern chaser, looking expectantly at Walker.

"Not yet," Walker said to him. "Not yet, but soon enough."

The stranger continued to fire periodically. It was almost two hours later before Walker saw what might have been a round from the stranger fall into the sea about fifty yards aft and off to starboard.

He turned to Cannon. "Fire as your gun bears, a few ranging shots."

There was little chance that they would hit anything, but the men would at least be encouraged by the sound of their own gunfire. Cannon pulled the tompion out from under the gun to achieve the greatest elevation and used a marlinspike to edge the gun's aim directly at the stranger. He picked up the firing lanyard and, bracing himself against the wind, stood off to one side, waiting for the stern to rise to its highest point. As it did, he pulled the lanyard.

The flintlock sparked and flashed, and the long nine went off with a satisfying bang, jumping back inboard as the wind whipped the white smoke forward. Cannon's mates hauled on the tackles to bring it all the way in, swabbed the barrel, reloaded and hauled the gun back outboard. Cannon pulled the lanyard as the stern again rose to its highest point.

After another shot, Walker called a halt. "That'll do for now."

The gun crew reloaded, ran the gun out, and secured it.

As the stranger edged closer, the darkness behind them spread to the south and north and rose higher in the sky. Under and within that darkness were winds far stronger than those that drove them ahead now.

The sun, which had shone only briefly, was now hidden by a dark gray overcast.

"That weather is moving faster than the two of us now," Mink shouted over the wind. "It'll be a near thing if he gets to us before it gets to him,"

"Aye," Walker replied, his back to the wind. "And it will be upon us almost as fast."

Hours passed under threatening skies. The stranger continued both to fire upon and gain on them. Walker ordered Cannon to resume firing when it became apparent that the stranger's shots were starting to fall within range. It was not long before one of those shots finally hit home, striking the mizzen's aft topping lift.

The events of the next few minutes happened so quickly that it seemed to Walker, when he looked back on them, that they had happened almost simultaneously. When the aft topping lift let go, it put so great a strain on the forward topping lift that, in seconds, it failed, sending the gaff down and forward and unbalancing the ship, sending her slightly to starboard. With winds howling, Walker turned his attention to getting the ship back on course but failed to see that a topping lift block had come loose and was falling onto the quarterdeck. It would have struck him if Jessup had not appeared and, throwing his weight into Walker, pushed him out of its way, only to have it strike a glancing blow on Jessup himself. Walker managed to catch himself on the forward quarterdeck railing and turned to see Mink dragging Jessup across the deck.

Mink shouted over the wind to Walker, "I'll get him below."

Before Walker could fully process what had happened, Cannon pointed astern and shouted to him, "He's going down."

And indeed he was. The stranger, with every possible sail set, was finally and suddenly overtaken by the worst of the storm's winds and was slowly rolling onto his starboard side. The wind, Walker realized, must have sheered in from his port side. The men on the quarterdeck stared transfixed as the roll continued, but Walker knew that those same raging winds would be on them quickly. Their only hope of survival was to reduce the ship's windage, the total area exposed to the wind, so that she would not be driven down as the stranger had.

He turned and shouted forward, "Loose all sheets, loose all sheets." And to Stark, "Ease your helm to starboard."

Word was passed along the deck over the howls of the wind. The men hesitated only momentarily at the strange order before training and discipline bore fruit and, led by Darling, they cast off the sheets, the ropes attached to the foot, the lower edge of each sail that kept the them taut and drawing wind. They were barely done when the full force of the storm, with heavier wind and driving rain, overtook the ship. Even with the sheets loosed, the rigging and the great mass of canvas flapping in the wind still created emough windage to drive her forward and down. Bringing the helm to starboard meant that the wind, which had taken the stranger on the port side and rolled her starboard, drove the *Barbadoes* forward, pressing her bow down but holding her balanced on an almost even keel. As her bow went down, she picked up a wall of blue water with her foredeck and tossed it aft, rolling it down the deck as the bow rose again. The men on the upper deck wrapped their arms around the standing rigging, railings, spare spars, anything that afforded a good grip. Walker and the men on the quarterdeck held to the forward railing as the powerful wave washed over them.

Walker struggled to his feet. Stark and the men at the helm had managed to keep the little ship before the wind. A few men had been pulled loose by the wave and thrown back against the bulkhead that formed the forward wall of Walker's cabin. They wouldn't know if anyone had been washed overboard until the storm abated and they could muster the men.

The worst of the storm continued for the next two hours, driving them forward and to the east of their chosen course. Once they had steadied the ship, the business of cleaning up the rigging began. Men struggled aloft and edged out along the footropes to haul in and furl the sails, no mean feat in this wind when the phrase, 'one hand for yourself and one for the ship' took on a special meaning. The stunsails had been damaged to the extent that here was little to do but cut them and their rigging loose and let them blow off into the storm. When the men were done, the ship ran forward under topsails and a closely reefed mizzen.

After a time, the storm turned to the north, the seas began to moderate, and the skies brightened noticeably. Mink had the watch. Walker had not left the quarterdeck. He was cold and his legs ached from standing. He walked to the ladder that led to the deck and sat down on the top step. The men had done a remarkable job of putting the ship to rights. There was still much to do, but the rigging was secured--in many places jury rigged, but secure and functioning.

Mink walked to the base of the ladder and spoke over the wind, "What say you to resuming our original course? I think the seas will let us get in some northing now. And as soon as we can get a fix, we'll correct for the miles we've been driven to the east."

"Make it so," Walker shouted back. "And see if we can get the galley fires lighted. The men will be wanting a hot meal, and rum."

Mink waved his assent and began to shout orders. The men at the wheel eased the ship to port as the men braced the yards around to set her on the old course, and an idler hurried below to rouse out the cook.

Eight bells rang. Time to change the watch. As the watch shifted, one of Stark's mates relieved him. Walker smiled as Stark went below. If Stark would allow himself to be relieved, then they must indeed be out of danger.

Jessup had been on Walker's mind this whole time. He made his way to the after companionway and down to the gun deck. Damage here, he noted, appeared to have been mimimal. Some shot had come loose from the ready racks, but the guns had remained secure, a good thing, for the damage a loose cannon could do rolling about a deck was incalculable. He continued on down to the orlop deck, the light diminishing as he did. He stood for a moment at the foot of the ladder to let his eyes adjust to the dark and stooped down to avoid hitting his head on the deck beams above him.

The orlop was lighted with lanterns that hung from the overhead. They cast shifting dark shadows of Hipple and his assistants as they moved about. Jessup lay on a cot furthest from the companion ladder. Three other men were also in Hipple's charge. Jessup had his eyes closed, apparently asleep.

Hipple approached Walker. "Your servant's got himself an awful bruise and I've no doubt some cracked or broken ribs. There's little to do for it but to bind him up as I've done and let him rest. It will heal on its own. I've given him laudanum for the pain. He'll sleep for a bit now."

"And the others?"

"Two badly strained shoulders and a broken arm. Again, nothing that time and care will not heal."

"Thank you," Walker said. He went to the other three men, asked after their injuries, and promised them an extra tot of rum for their troubles, the seaman's cure for everything.

Before he left, he sat by Jessup, who snored softly as he slept. Once again, Walker marveled that Jessup had appeared just when he was needed. He knew full well that it would be himself lying in that cot, or worse, if Jessup had not shoved him from under the falling block.

After a few minutes, he returned to the quarterdeck. The sky had brightened noticeably since he had gone below, and the seas had contined to moderate. They were free of the storm. Mink was staring aft.

"No sign of him, eh?" Walker asked.

"None," Mink replied. "Nothing since he started to roll. My God, how awful. One moment you're sailing, and the next you're on your beam ends, sinking."

"So you think he went down?" Walker asked.

"I do," Mink replied, turning to Walker. "Can you imagine recovering from that angle? His starboard rail had to have been under by then. Everything stored below would be shifting to starboard, as well."

"No, I'm sure you're right."

"What about the survivors? If there were any?"

"You mean should we look for them?" Walker looked aft again. "In other circumstances, I would. But we don't know where we were he went down, and we don't really know where we are now. I'm afraid it would come to nothing more than days wasted, as much as I hate to say it and in spite of how callous it sounds."

"Don't give it more thought," Mink said. "We have a mission. It makes no sense to interrupt it when the chance of finding survivors is less than the chance of finding where she went down."

The galley fires had been lighted. The smell of boiling beef wafted up from below. The call of "Up spirits" signaled it was time for the daily rum ration, another sign that things were returning to normal.

"Will you join me in my cabin, Samuel? If there hasn't been too much damage, we should be able to put a meal together."

"With pleasure," Mink answered.

Walker's cabin was surprisingly orderly. Arthur and Andrew, who stood at attention by the port side alcove, had put it to rights and had anticipated Walker. A dinner for two of preserved meats and cheese with a bottle of wine was laid out on the table.

"Jessup has trained you both well," Walker said. "This is excellent work."

"Thank you, sir," they both said in unison, and Arthur added, "If you please, sir, how is Mr. Jessup?"

"He's banged up pretty good, but the surgeon tells me that time and rest will see him put to rights. You may visit him in the orlop, but I'd wait until tomorrow. He's sleeping now."

"Yes, sir, thank you, sir," Arthur said. "And let us know when you'll be wanting your coffee, sirs." With that, they disappeared into the pantry.

The two men eased themselves into their chairs, and Mink poured two glasses of wine. They were both tired from lack of sleep and for having been on their feet for hours on end, so many that they had lost count. And they were hungry. They ate and drank in silence for a few minutes until Colins stepped into the cabin.

"Mr. Talbot's compliments, sir," he said, "and the muster shows all are accounted for."

"Thank you, Colins," Walker replied. "Tell him we will be up when we are finished our meal."

"Aye, sir," Colins said, and he closed the door behind him. Mink cut off a bit of cheese and washed it down with a sip of wine. "Up after our meal? It's getting on to evening. Hadn't you better rest? You look as tired as I feel, and I would not wish that on anyone."

"Tired, yes. But I want to sort out where we are. I'll sleep better knowing that."

"Surely, but there's no way to do that now. The sky's still overcast. Besides, I'm sure Stark will have a dead reckoning based on his estimates of our speed and direction over the past hours, and that's good enough for me, for now. Have your coffee and sleep. I've the next watch, but I'll still have time for a few hours below before it. It will be dark by then, and I'll wake you the moment there are stars enough to work with."

Walker paused a moment, looked out the stern windows at the overcast sky, and turned back to Mink.

"Very well, you convince me. Let us both sleep until your watch. Arthur, Andrew, coffee if you please."

They finished their coffee, and Mink left for his cabin in the gun room. Walker slipped out of his jacket and handed it to Arthur as Andrew cleared the table. Walker was asleep as his head touched the pillow. Andrew covered him with a blanket.

Mink decided to look in on Jessup before he turned in. He stepped off the ladder in the orlop and greeted Hipple, who briefed him on the injuries as he had Walker. Jessup still slept. Mink spent some time with the three seamen before he went and sat by Jessup. After a moment or two, Jessup awoke and looked at Mink through slightly unfocused eyes.

"Mr. Mink?"

"Aye," Mink replied. "How are you feeling?"

Jessup looked away, then back to Mink and said, "You have to watch after your boys, you know. That's what my mother said. You have to watch after your boys. They're the ones who'll get in trouble, not the girls."

The laudanum had let Jessup's servant's voice slip into a country accent that Mink could not quite place. Jessup looked around again, blinked his eyes, looked back to Mink and went on, "The girls will take care of themselves, mother said. It's your boys who'll need looking after, she told us." He paused, looked around again, and asked, "I looked after him, did I not? He's well?" There was genuine concern on his voice.

"You did," Mink said. "You looked after him. He's well. He's been to see you. He worries over you."

"As I over him." Jessup closed his eyes. Speaking was tiring.

Hipple approached. "He needs his rest, sir, if you please."

"Yes, of course," Mink replied. He rose and stood stooped under the deck beams for a minute, looking at Jessup, who began to snore softly again.

XXXIII

Walker awoke some minutes before the next watch and glanced at the tell-tale compass above his head. They still held the same course they had set as they emerged from the storm.

He lay there listening to the sounds of the ship, the creaking of the timbers as they flexed and relaxed, driven through a following sea.

The sentry stomped, and the door opened. Mink entered the cabin. "Come along. I'm about to relieve Talbot. The clouds are gone, and we've our pick of the stars."

"Go. I'll join you presently," Walker answered. As he swung his feet onto the deck, Arthur appeared with a cloth soaked in warm water and a cup of hot coffee. Andrew stood next to him with a clean shirt and a fresh jacket. Arthur put the coffee on the table and approached Walker.

"If you please, sir," he said as he began to unbutton Walker's shirt. Walker stripped off the shirt and scrubbed his upper body with the wet, warm cloth. Arthur handed him a dry cloth to towel himself with.

As he put on the clean shirt Arthur said, "And your hair, sir. It's gone adrift a bit, sir. Sit here for a moment will you?" indicating his chair by the table. Walker sat and sipped coffee as Arthur gathered his hair and tied it behind him with a blue ribbon. As Arthur tied off the bow, Andrew held out the jacket. Walker slipped it on and went out on deck to the stomping of the marine sentry coming to attention. Routine had returned to the ship.

The sky had cleared, and, as Mink had said, they had their pick of the stars. With Stark, they set to the business of determining their position.

It turned out that Stark's dead reckoning estimate was not very far off the mark. They adjusted course slightly to the north. If the wind held steady, they were about two weeks out from Portsmouth.

They spent the next few days putting the ship fully to rights, replacing the jury rigs with proper rigging, swapping out worn sails for new, and touching up the paint.

XXXIV

On the fourth day, Walker awoke at dawn to Colins standing next to his cot.

"Mr. Mink's compliments, sir, and there is a strange sail to starboard."

"Thank you, Colins," Walker replied as he rose quickly, took his telescope from its rack, and headed out the door, with Arthur trailing close behind with his coat. He stood by the binnacle and listened to Mink's report as Arthur helped him into the coat.

"She's not quite visible from the deck," Mink said, "but, from her topgallants, lookout thinks she could be a small frigate."

"Clear for action while I go have a look." Walker replied. Mink gave the order as Walker headed for the startboard ratlines.

McCann was lookout that watch. He didn't have to point to the ship, her topgallants were clearly visible to starboard.

"Mornin', sir," McCann said.

"Good morning, McCann," Walker replied as he unlimbered his telescope. "What do you think of this fellow?"

"Small frigate, could be. Bearing hasn'a changed since I first seen her. And you can see a bit more of her targallans now than ye could at first light."

A closer look didn't tell Walker much more than McCann had. The ship appeared to be a small frigate, and, from the position of her masts, she was on a converging course. If the bearing did not change, they would come together some time in the next hour or so. Remembering his orders, Walker considered running from her. She was, however, hardly a superior force, and the only way to avoid her was to turn north with her on his heels, driving him away from England. No, it looked as if this would be a fight.

Walker watched the strange ship for about five more minutes to confirm his original observations before he returned to the deck, exchanging greetings on his way down with the marines that were already at their battle station in the maintop.

By the time Walker stepped onto the deck again, the ship was fully cleared for action. Gun crews manned their guns, sand had been strewn across the decks to give bare-footed men traction in the blood that could soon cover them. Pistols and cutlasses had been distributed to the crew. Mink, Talbot, and Stark were waiting for him at the binnacle. Darling and Cannon stood a few paces behind them. Andrew was also there with a hot cup of coffee.

Walker took a sip of coffee and spoke to them, "She looks to be a small frigate, on a converging course. We should be upon her in the next hour. We will assume she is French and that we are at war with them again until we prove otherwise."

"And what if she is and we are?" Talbot asked.

Walker looked at Mink. "What was it Nelson said? 'Just go at them,' wasn't it?"

"But what does that mean?" Talbot asked.

Mink answered, "Just what it says, go straight at them, guns blazing, board them, and take them."

"In other words," Walker added, "Don't waste time, shot, and powder standing off and trading broadsides with them. Attack them, engage them close in. It's a particularly good strategy if you can catch the enemy off guard, unbalance him a bit. At any rate, it is what we shall plan for if he let's us get close enough."

Walker turned to Darling and Cannon. "You heard all that. Cannon, be sure your gun captains understand that we value rate of fire over accuracy in this encounter. We want to throw a lot of iron at them to keep them off balance."

Cannon nodded, "Aye, sir."

"And Darling, the men and the port side gun crews will make up the initial boarding party, but be sure to keep out of sight as much as possible until the last minute."

"Aye," Darling replied with a knuckle to his forehard.

"Off with you then, and good luck."

As the two men turned to leave, Walker turned to Mink. "We have time for breakfast. Will you join me?

"I will," Mink replied.

The ship's company had already eaten, and the galley fires, including Walker's small stove, were out, so, of necessity, breakfast was cold meat and cheese. As they sat down, Arthur brought in a fresh pot of hot coffee. Mink cut himself a piece of cheese and chewed on it as he attacked a piece of hardtack with strawberry preserve in what he knew would be a vain attempt to soften it. Walker swallowed a bit of preserved pheasant and washed it down with coffee.

Mink put the hardtack down and turned to Walker. "We have, so far, avoided a fight, as your orders direct. Why are we taking this fellow on now, when we're so close to home?"

"If he hadn't been so close when the sun came up, I might have shown him our heels. But getting away at that point would have been an awkward business, and I'm not at all certain that we wouldn't have been in for a fight after all. As to our orders, they state we are to avoid 'superior forces.' This fellow looks to be an even match, at best. And besides, if we sail into Portsmount with the gold and a prize, no one at the Admiralty is going to quibble about the wording of our orders."

"Aye that," Mink laughed.

Walker changed the subject. "So tell me, Samuel, what do you think of this lot as fighting men? I'd wager that not one in four of them has even been in a tavern brawl, no less a bit of hand to hand with a cutlass on a ship's deck."

"No doubt, but circumstances often make the man. They have a clear enemy, no place to run, and I think we've trained them properly. I think they'll acquit themselves quite well."

"Then let us go find out. I wanted to be off the deck for a bit so they didn't think I was fretting over this. But now it's time to be master and commander."

As the two men got up from the table, Andrew took Walker's sword from the rack and went to strap it on him.

Walker stopped him, "The cutlass lad. Swords are fine decorations, but now there's work to be done."

Jessup had not only had the armorer put a good edge on Walker's old cutlass, he had also had the sailmaker fashion a leather scabbard for it. Walker hung the strap over his left shoulder so that the scabbard hung at his right side where he could easily draw the cutlass with his left hand. This would not have been possible with his sword which, by custom, hung from the left hip.

X X X V

They were still closing on the other ship, but it appeared to have altered course slightly. Stark confirmed this. "She looks to have edged a bit to the east, sir. She's not running off, for sure, but maybe she wants a better look at us before she commits to anything."

They were not yet hull-down to each other, but the time for action was drawing near. Walker began to walk to the after companionway. "Come along, Samuel, let us see how the men are getting on."

Sunlight filtered through the gangways and spare spars that covered the forward part of the gun deck. Cannon stood by the mainmast. The men manning the starboard guns were at their guns. The port gun crews had gathered at the forward and aft gangways, armed and ready to go on deck.

Walker spoke to them from near the mainmast. "Men, we are approaching what we believe is a French warship. And it is all too possible that we are at war with France once again. If we are, we will fight this ship, and we will force her to surrender. We don't want to sink her because no prize court will buy a sunken vessel."

This elicited a few laughs.

"To force her surrender, we will throw iron at her faster than she can return it, and we will go straight for her, boarding her as quickly as we can. You men on the starboard guns, give us rapid fire over accuracy to keep the enemy off balance. The rest of you stay below until you are called. We don't want to let on how many of you there are until the last minute. When you are told to go, go quickly. Board her, make noise, yell, and brandish your weapons before you to unman them, cause them to drop their weapons, and surrender."

Walker paused for a moment, drew his cutlass and held it as high as he could in the low overhead of the gun deck. "What say you men? For England!"

"For England! For England!" came the enthusiastic replies, punctuated by the clattering of cutlasses against each other and the deck. The men continued to cheer as they made their way back to the after companionway.

As they reached the main deck Mink commented, "I think you've got this master and commander thing going quite well for someone who's only been at it such a short time."

"You do, honestly?"

"I do. I think all that cheering and banging of cutlasses showed genuine enthusiasm."

"Well," Walker replied, pointing off to starboard, "we'll know soon enough. Our friend is almost hull down."

They studied the stranger for a few minutes before Mink said, "Let me go have a closer look." He started for the starboard ratlines and was back in a few minutes. "Looks to be one of their 24-gun, 12-pounder frigates. Word has it that they're lighty built, sacrificing strength for speed."

"If that's so," Walker replied, "then our nine-pounders may do her some real damage."

In the time it had taken Mink to get aloft and back down, the other ship had neared to the point that they could see her rail and the tops of her gun ports.

Stark interrupted, "Sir, she's come west a bit. Looks as if she's decided to give us a closer look."

"Or to engage," Walker replied. "It's time to find out." He called to the signals midshipman, "Hoist the ensign, the largest we have. I don't want our friend to mistake us for someone else."

The ensign was soon flying from the peak of the mizzen gaff. A few minutes after it broke out, the strange ship hoisted the tricolor of France.

"Well," Walker said, "that tells us half of what we need to know."

No sooner had she had identified herself than the Frenchman's gun ports flew up, and she fired a broadside.

"And that," Mink replied, "tells us the other half."

The shots that didn't fall short were wide.

"That's just sloppy business," Mink continued, "barely in range and poorly aimed. If he can't do better than that with his first broadside, our odds of taking him just rose a point or two."

Walker was looking at his watch when the second, somewhat ragged broadside went off. "A little over four minutes. Our crews had it down to two to three minutes, as I recall."

"Aye," Mink replied, "Never over three in any case."

"Pass the word to Cannon that he may fire when he has the range and then continue to fire as his guns bear."

Several balls from the third broadside hit the *Barbadoes'* hull but did little damage.

"She's solidly built. The Yanks did a fine job on her. Seasoned oak and properly fastened." Mink was referring to the all too common practice of British shipbuilders to use green timber and a minimum of bolts and nails to save money.

A third broadside was not much more effective than the first two. It was then that Cannon decided he had the range. The starboard gunports flew up, the nine-pounders rolled into place and fired as one. Splinters flew all along the Frenchman's side as cheers rose from the gun deck. The two ships then settled down to firing at each other, the Frenchman in broadsides, the *Barbadoes* as her individual guns could be reloaded and brought to bear.

Walker and Mink stood near the binnacle with Talbot and Stark. Talbot did his best not to duck as cannonballs and rifle shot flew near them. The others ignored them. The two ships were still on converging courses, but *Barbadoes* had been sailing a bit faster and was a little ahead of her opponent.

Walker turned to Stark and shouted over the roar of the cannon, "I make it that if we can gain a half length on her, we can come to starboard and close. What say you?"

"Aye," Stark shouted. "A few more minutes of this."

As they began to edge ahead of the Frenchman and close on her, she started to bear away to starboard as if she sensed Walker's plan. As she did this, the ship lost some way as her crew were slow to trim the sails.

Darling's men were on top of the course change, so, as *Barbadoes* swung to starboard, she bore down on the enemy. They could see a sudden flurry of activity on the Frenchman as they realized what Walker was up to. Stark brought the ship further to starboard. They were at fifty yards and closing fast. Walker gave the signal that brought the first wave of boarders up onto the main deck. They ran from the companionways to crouch along the rail under the hammock nettings, out of sight of the opposing ship. Mink and Talbot were to lead them, Mink forward and Talbot aft. They looked to Walker, waiting for a signal.

When Stark's "a few more minutes" had passed, they had gained enough on the Frenchman that he looked to Walker. Walker nodded his assent, and Stark ordered the wheel to starboard. At the same time, he ordered the guns to cease firing. The enemy's guns had ceased. There was confusion on the Frenchman's main deck as it became clear that she was about to be boarded. She tried again to swing to starboard, but it was too late. Just before the two ships collided, grapnels flew from the *Barbadoes*, and the lines attached to them were drawn tight to keep the ships from drifting apart.

Mink, at the bow, waved his cutlass over his head and shouted to the boarders, "Now! Have at them!" as he, joined by Talbot at the stern, leapt across to the other ship.

The men followed, climbing over the hammock nettings waving their weapons and shouting. A general melee ensued.

Walker saw Talbot fall but get back on his feet quickly to rejoin the fight, bleeding from his left arm. The Frenchmen at first held their ground but then retreated, regrouped, and tried to advance again. But it quickly turned into a rout as the second wave of boarders swarmed up from the gun deck and joined the fight. The unprepared Frenchmen were driven back to their starboard rail and, as Walker had predicted, were unmanned. Despite the urging of their officers, they began to drop their weapons and show their hands.

Finally, the French captain shouted to Walker in French and English, "Je frappe mon Drapeau! I strike my flag! I strike!" The tricolor slowly began to descend from the peak of the Frenchman's mizzen.

Barbadoes' marines, under Mink's direction, took charge of the French prisoners as the men collected their weapons. Mink confronted the French captain and his first lieutenant and escorted them aboard the *Barbadoes*.

Walker sheathed his cutlass as the French captain approached him and saluted. "I am Henri Deschamps, captain of the frigate *Nymphe*. This is my lieutenant, Auguste Levesque."

The two Frenchmen were dressed in full formal uniforms, adorned with gold braid and brass buttons, in stark contrast to Walker's simple white-faced jacket and single epaulette. As he saluted, Deschamps glanced down, taking notice of Walker's bare feet.

Deschamps began to unhook his sword from its belt to offer it to Walker as a formal sign of surrender.

Walker raised his hands in refusal. "If you will give me your parole, you may keep your sword. You fought well."

"Merci, capitaine," Deschamps responded. "You have my assurance."

Walker chose not to point out that he was a commander, not a captain. The more rank he held in their eyes the better for the present.

"Lieutenant Mink will show you to your quarters. I will ask you to join me in my cabin after I have seen to my men and my ship."

"But, capitaine," Deschamps protested, "I, also, am concerned for my men and my ship. Perhaps I might . . ."

Walker cut him short, "I have no less concern for your men and your ship than I have for mine. I will see to them. For now, I ask that you accompany Lieutenant Mink."

Deschamps hesitated, then saluted and turned to Mink who led the way to the gun room, with two marines following closely behind.

Walker surveyed the two ships. There was a good deal of damage to both, but much of it on the *Barbadoes* appeared superficial. The Frenchman looked to have gotten the worst of it. Darling was already putting parties from both ships to work setting the rigging to rights. Talbot approached Walker, his upper left arm tied in a bloody, makeshift bandage.

"Talbot, you are not badly injured?" Walker questioned.

"No sir. I was struck down but managed to get to my feet. The wound is not deep."

Mink rejoined him. "The French gentlemen are in separate staterooms with marines outside their doors."

"Good," Walker replied, "And the butcher's bill?"

"I don't have a final total, but I had a look about for injuires, and it seems there are two dead on the Frenchie, a few serious wounds, and a good lot of less serious splinter and cutlass wounds. Our butcher's bill will be quite short, no deaths but, again, a good bit of mostly minor splinter and cutlass wounds, like Talbot here," Mink turned to Talbot. "So, you've been blooded, eh?"

"That I have," Talbot replied. "That I have."

"And you fought well," Walker said.

Mink grinned and squeezed Talbot's shoulder on his uninjured side. "Aye, you did well."

Talbot managed a smile. "Thank you."

"Now, go find Mr. Hipple, and get that properly bandaged," Walker said. "I want you to assume command of the prize."

"Sir?" Talbot said, surprised. Then with a smile, "Yes sir, thank you, sir."

As Talbot walked off to find Hipple, Walker turned to Mink. "What do you think? Did I make the right call?"

"Indeed, I think you did. He's learned a lot on this voyage, and a taste of command will serve him well. Might I suggest we send Darling with him? An experienced hand at his side might be of some use."

"Good thought. Make it so."

The next two hours were occupied in tending to the wounded, burying the dead, and getting the two ships ready to sail. Walker also transferred some of the crew of the *Nymphe* aboard the *Barbadoes,* including the senior petty officers, the thinking being that the fewer senior men left aboard, the less the chance that the crew might try to retake the ship. Colins played an important part in this because, after he revealed that he spoke a passable French, Walker decided to add him to the prize crew. There were a number among the French crew who spoke English, but a loyal translator would be a great help to Talbot.

They got underway with a few hours of sunlight left. Lanterns were to be hung in a certain pattern in the rigging on both ships to enable them to keep track of each other at night. Talbot was to fire a gun if things got out of hand and to stay under *Barbadoes'* lee so that she could move quickly to assist him. A contingent of *Barbadoes'* marines were placed aboard *Nymphe.*

XXXVI

The next few days were uneventful. *Nymphe* sailed under *Barbadoes'* lee as a southwest breeze carried them toward Land's End. As they entered the Channel, they spoke with an aviso that was returning from the blockade fleet to Portsmouth. The aviso would get there well ahead of them, so Walker penned a note to the superintendent of the yard, advising him that he would be arriving with prisoners and a prize, and that he had a small cargo that required "discretion and special handling."

The aviso got to Portsmouth sufficiently ahead of Walker that word had spread of his prize, the first prize, he would later discover, of the renewed war.

Cheers rang out from the ships at anchor and men on the shore. Several guns were fired as *Barbadoes* shepherded her slightly larger and more heavily gunned *Nymphe* into the harbor, the white ensign fluttering over the tricolor at her mizzen peak.

Guard boats led the two ships to their anchorages. As soon as their anchors had set, several launches set out to them, all but one went to the French ship where they began to disembark prisoners. The other launch pulled alongside *Barbadoes*. The superindent of the yard, Sir James Selfridge, was in the sternsheets. Walker greeted him at the entryport. They had met before when the ship was fitting out.

"It was good of you come personally, sir," Walker said as they shook hands. "You remember my first lieutenant, Samuel Mink?"

Selfridge took Mink's hand. "Of course, a pleasure to see you again, sir."

When the formalities were done, Walker suggested they continue their conversation in his cabin. As they started there, Selfridge congratulated Walker, "You probably do not know that you have captured the first prize of the renewed hostilities."

"I did not sir," Walker said, a bit taken aback by the knowledge while Mink smiled and swelled a bit.

"And to top it, you've taken a warship of at least equal strength."

"Truth be told," Walker replied, "we discovered in conversation with her captain that the *Nymphe* was a bit undermanned and with more raw hands than I would like to sail with."

"Possibly, but that does not change the fact that she is here and that you have all the credit for bringing her here. Oh," Selfridge continued with a smile, "and you also have all the prize money as I understand that you were on an independent mission." This was true. *Barbadoes* was not attached to any fleet so there was no admiral to share the prize money with.

"Indeed," was all Walker could manage in reply. The promise of prize money had not yet occurred to him, while Mink had already calculated his likely share.

They had reached his cabin door. He turned to the marine sentry. "Pass the word for Mister Holdsworth and Mister Cannon." With a stomp of his boot and a voice that could be heard in London, the sentry let Holdsworth and Cannon know that they were wanted in the captain's cabin.

Jessup had laid out a decanter and glasses. Mink poured. Selfridge raised his glass. "To your success, commander." They drank and toasted again, "To the King."

Selfridge got to the point, "So, commander, you should know that the Admiralty advised me that you might request my confidential assistance. What is it that requires discretion in this matter?"

"Gold, sir. It is gold."

Before Selfridge could react, Holdsworth and Cannon were at the door.

"Holdsworth," Walker said, "fetch some tools, we want open those crates. And Cannon, give us a hand rousting them out."

Holdsworth went back on deck and returned with a hammer and prybar. Selfridge watched as Walker, Mink, and Cannon unlashed the three crates and brought them to the center of the cabin.

As Holdsworth began to remove their tops, Walker explained, "We were under admiralty orders to attempt to locate a certain amount of gold. My orders forbid me to go into any detail, but, as you can see, we were successful."

Holdsworth had the top off the first crate and was working on the second. Selfridge bent down, picked up one of the gold bars, and hefted it. "Good heavens," he exclaimed, "this is a fortune."

"Yes, it is a substantial amount," Walker replied. "I have been instructed by their lordships to place this in your hands for safekeeping until they contact you."

"Yes, of course. I shall keep it under guard."

"Good, thank you," Walker replied as he walked to Perkins' desk and retrieved a document. "I have taken the liberty of having my clerk draw up a receipt. All it requires is that we insert the quantity of bars. Shall we count them together?"

When the count was complete, Selfridge and Walker signed the receipt, and Mink made a fair copy that both of them signed. The crates were lowered into Selfridge's barge, and he was away. In taking his leave, Selfridge assured Walker that the full resources of the yard would be at his disposal to repair and refit his ship.

"Well," Mink said as the barge pulled away, "that is a great load off my mind."

"Mine as well," Walker replied. "Mine as well."

The rest of that day and the next were spent in assessing what damage had not yet been repaired, what supplies they needed to refit for sea, and what departments of the yard needed to be "encouraged" in order to gain their cooperaton. *Barbadoes,* they discovered was exceptionally sturdily built. She had suffered surprisingly little damage in her encounter with *Nymphe.* They expected her to be ready for sea in relatively short order.

On the third day, Walker and Mink left by carriage for London to report to Burns. Arthur and Andrew accompanied them. Jessup was well on the mend by now, but still too sore to sit a carriage on the road for any amount of time.

X X X V I I

The carriage rolled to a stop in front of the Walker home. Walker and Mink stepped down and waited as Arthur and Andrew retrieved their bags from the boot. Without Jessup in the house, no one opened the door as they approached it. It was locked. Walker rang. After a moment's wait, it was opened by a young man, dressed as a butler, whom Walker did not recognize.

"May I help you, sir?" The young man said, looking slightly down his nose.

"I am Albert Walker. I live here."

The young man stared at Walker for a second before jumping aside, opening the door wide, and motioning them in with a bow and a sweep of his arm. As Walker entered the main hall, a woman's voice called out, "Albert, what are you doing here? I was told you were at sea."

She stood on the stairs, a few steps from the bottom. She was slightly taller than women of her time. She wore her light brown hair up, exposing a slender neck. Her hazel eyes sparkled.

Walker turned and smiled. "Isadora, indeed I was, but we are home only for a day or two, and then we are off to Portsmouth and to sea again."

She hurried to kiss and embrace him. Then she stood back and, turning to Mink, said, "And who could this possibly be?"

Mink stood and stared at her, quite at a loss for words.

Walker replied, "Isadora, may I present my good friend and comrade in arms, Samuel Mink. Samuel, my sister Isadora."

Isadora extended her hand with an amused smile. Mink continued to stare silently for another long second before he recovered himself, took her hand and made a leg.

"So this is the famous Lieutenant Mink," Isadora said. "Albert has told me much about you. I am honored."

"And I am delighted to finally meet you, Miss Walker. Albert has told me much about you, but his words did not come near to doing justice to your charms. I am captivated," Mink replied, making a quick recovery and turning on charms of his own.

Their eyes met in a mutual smile before Isadora curtsied and replied, "Such a good friend of Albert must not call me Miss Walker. You will call me Isadora, and I shall call you Samuel."

Mink nodded and, with a smile, said, "We shall make it so."

Walker watched all this, amused. Isadora had this effect on men, but he was surprised at Mink's reaction. He had never seen Mink at a loss with a woman.

Isadora turned back to Walker. "But where is Jessup? They said he was with you."

"Yes, he is," Walker replied. "He's back on the ship, recovering from some bad bruises and a cracked rib or two he suffered in saving my life. He will be fine, but he's still too sore to travel."

"Injured? But why on earth did you take him? Jessup is no seaman."

"It was no idea of mine," Walker said defensively. "I asked him to find servants for me and thought no more of it until it was time to board the carriage for Portsmouth, and there he was, packed and dressed for the road with two of Mrs. Anson's nephews to assist him. It was too late to make other arrangements. And I cannot say that he is no seaman. He was all too comfortable moving about the ship from the very first. But what are you doing here? I thought you would be in the country still."

Isadora stepped aside to clear the way to the stairs for them. "I will tell you, and you must tell me all about Jessup and the rest of your voyage. But first, you'll want to freshen up from the road, and it is almost time for dinner. Go, then. Meet me in the dining room."

When they got to their rooms, Arthur and Andrew had already laid out fresh uniforms and were just bringing in jugs of hot water for each of them to wash with.

XXXVIII

By the time Walker came back down the stairs, Mink was already in the dining room in conversation with Isadora. Carrying a canvas envelope with his log and the supplement, Walker went to the desk in the drawing room. There, he penned a note to Burns telling him they were back in London and requesting a meeting at the admiral's convenience. He sealed it and the canvas envelope and pulled the bell rope. The same young man who had answered the front door appeared in the drawing room.

"Ah, Walker said, and you are…?"

"Benson, sir, James Benson. And I must beg your pardon for the way I greeted you sir, I--"

Walker cut him short, "Think no more of it. You had no way of knowing who I was. You acted quite appropriately."

Benson was visibly relieved as Walker continued, "Now, Benson, I have a task for you. You are to take this canvas parcel and this note to Whitehall. When you step inside the doors, a porter will greet you." Walker reached into the pocket of his waistcoat and produced a coin. "Hand him the note and the canavs envelope with this coin held under your thumb so that he can see it. Tell him it is for Admiral Burns with Commander Walker's compliments, and be sure to tell him that you are instructed to await a reply."

"Yes sir, for Admiral Burns with your compliments, and I'm to wait on a reply."

"Exactly," Walker said. "Now off with you, make haste."

Benson turned toward the front door as Walker entered the dining room.

Isadora and Mink sat facing each other. Walker took his seat between them at the head of the table.

"Samuel has been telling me all about your exploits. Albert, you are a hero."

"Hardly, Isadora. I did my duty and could not have done it without Samuel and the rest of the crew."

"Nonetheless, you did wonderful things and you should be proud of it. Oh, and before I forget, the Duchess of Kent is having a do this evening. I've asked Samuel, and he has graciously agreed to escort me, if that is all right with you. Will you join us?"

"Of course that is all right with me. I have no say over what either of you do with your time. But go without me. I want to rest and turn in early."

"Albert, I urge you to reconsider. It is time that you mingle in society again. Two years have passed since the tragic loss of your dear Anna—"

Walker cut her off sharply. "I am well aware, Isadora, of how much time has passed since Anna's untimely death. And, if I were not, Samuel would surely remind me. Like you, he encourages me to-- how did you phrase it, Samuel? 'Mingle'?" He gazed at one then the other, noting their looks of concern. "I mean no offense and understand that you both wish me well. But I am not yet of a mind to be introduced to society's finest unmarried damsels. I prefer to retire early and rest."

"My brother may be stalwart at sea," Isadora smiled. "But in the company of ladies, he trembles."

"Not so, my sister." Walker's smile was almost imperceptible. "Though, indisputably, in the romantic arena, you have always fared better, being both more daring and more resilient than I."

"Have it your way then," Isadora replied, "but I think you, as the first and most gallant hero of this war, would easily be the centerpiece of the affair."

That was exactly what Walker hoped to avoid. He disliked being the center of attention anywhere and dreaded being hailed the hero at a soiree filled with young eager ladies.

They ate as Walker and Mink told Isadora the story of their journey, carefully avoiding any mention of the gold. In the middle of the meal,

Benson returned with a note from Burns, telling them that he would be pleased to see them the next day at three o'clock.

After dinner, Mink and Iadora set out to take a walk in the park across the street from the house. When Isadora excused herself to "freshen up," Walker took Mink into the drawing room and to the writing desk.

Walker lifted the top of the desk and took out Mink's flask, the one that had saved him from Jenkins' bullet. Walker had sent it off to be repaired before they left. It was now good as new and filled with Walker's best brandy.

Mink was not just surprised; he was genuinely touched. He took it from Walker and marveled at it. "This was my grandfather's, and I was sure it was lost forever. I don't know how to thank you."

"There's no need to thank me. It saved the life of my best friend, so surely it was worth saving."

"Indeed, indeed. But this was most thoughtful. Thank you."

Walker reached back into the desk and produced a flattened piece of lead. "And here is the bullet."

Mink laughed. "A good luck piece, no doubt."

Mink slipped the bullet and the flask into its pocket in his waistcoat. Then he paused. "See here, Albert, this business of my keeping company with Isadora, if I am in anyway overstepping--"

Walker cut him short. "Samuel, you are my best friend. I have no objection whatever. And as for Isadora, even my father has not been able to tell her what to do from the time she was a young girl. She is a very independent woman. She does as she pleases, and she is pleased to be with you. Give this no more thought, other than to gird yourself, being prepared for her capricious nature."

Just then they heard Isadora walk down the stairs, and they went out to meet her.

When Mink and Isadora had left, Walker took his his coffee and a book to read into the drawing room. Before he sat to read, though, stood at his desk, looking at a small door to a compartment. After a moment, he unlocked the door, opened the compartment, and removed the small silhouette of a lady.

How long it had been since he'd last viewed it, yet, even now, memories flooded back to him as fresh as if no time had passed. Her scent, her violet eyes. Dear Anna.

Staring at her profile, he entertained thoughts of how, if she had lived, he would have had a wife to return home to, likely a child, as well.

Perhaps he'd been wrong to stay at home alone. Well, home alone he was. And nothing was to be helped by further grieving. He replaced the shadow, locked the tiny compartment door, and sat beside the lamplight with his book. Before he could read a single page, he was asleep, snoring softly.

X X X I X

The next day at precisely three o'clock, Walker knocked on the door at the top of the spiral staircase. Forbes opened it and welcomed them inside.

Burns greeted them at the door to his chambers with a broad grin and warm handshakes, "Commander Walker, Lieutenant Mink, it is my great pleasure and honor to welcome you back. Congratulations to you both. Here, let me have your hats, and please have a seat."

Walker and Mink took chairs at Burns' desk while he put their hats on a shelf behind them.

"Thank you, sir," Walker said. "The pleasure is mine."

"And mine," Mink added."

"Not at all, not at all. You have accomplished your assigned missions and more, and we must celebrate." Burns poured three glasses from a decanter on a side table. "To your success."

They drank, and Burns sat behind his desk. "You have no idea yet what your bringing in that prize has done for your reputation and for the morale of both the Navy and the man on the street."

Barbadoes' log and Walker's supplemental report sat in front of Burns. Before Walker could respond, Burns picked them up and hefted them. "I have read these both several times and shared them with certain of their Lordships. We are all quite pleased with how this turned out. Not only did you accomplish both your missions, but you also solved the riddle of the *Diligence.* Then you survived a chase by a superior force, escaped a violent storm, and arrived with a French frigate under your lee as a prize. That is wonderful work."

"Thank you, sir," Walker said, "but as I pointed out in my report, the Frenchman was not fully manned."

"We saw that, and it was honest of you to point it out, but did you know it was undermanned when you attacked?"

"Why, no, sir, of course not. We were quite fortunate in that."

"And fortune favors the brave, does it not?" Burns said with a broad smile.

"Yes, sir," Walker smiled back. "That is what I have heard."

"Then no more about undermanned Frenchies. You attacked a superior force and captured it. That is what happened, and that is what the record will show."

Mink glanced at Walker with a bit of 'I told you so' on his face.

Burns took a quick sip of wine and continued, "And I must thank you for the kind words you had for my nephew regarding his conduct in that encounter."

"There is no need to thank me, sir. Charles earned those words. He led his men into the thick of the fight without hesitation. He's turning into a fine officer."

"Thank you. That is, of course, very good to hear. I shall pass your words on to his father. And your praise for young Colins did not go unnoticed. I took the liberty of passing that on to his father."

Burns leaned forward and put his arms on the desk before he continued, "Now then, something happened while you were away that has changed the game a bit, rearranged the chessmen on our little board, so to speak." He hesitated momentarily, "Jenkins is dead."

Mink sat up. "Dead sir? But his wound—"

Burns, leaning back in his chair, finished his sentence for him. "Was not serious, that was true. But just as he seemed to have recovered, it was found that he had developed a corruption in his blood. By the time it was discovered, it was too late to do anything for him. As we could find no family for him, no next of kin, he was buried quietly on the grounds of the asylum."

"So," Walker said, "officially, Jenkins disappeared on the way home from work one day and was never seen again."

"Exactly," Burns replied.

"But what of the people at Woolich? Certainly there are people there who were privy to this, or who heard about it?"

"Of course, but in time it will become no more than a rumor, which is mostly what it is now."

"And the gold never disappeared, and it was never recovered, so it cannot be considered a prize," Mink added, not quite managing to hide his disappointment.

"Precisely," Burns answered. "It would have made an interesting argument before the prize court that the gold was property taken and recovered, but we shall never know. But you two will have a nice settlement out of the French prize, and your taking of it will pay you dividends in the future that just may match what would have been your share of the gold."

Burns took a sip of wine as Walker looked to Mink and back to Burns. "And what of Holdsworth, sir? What's to become of him?"

"Ah, yes, Holdsdworth," Burns said, leaning back in his chair. "He was an apparently unwilling participant in the theft of the gold and unquestionably guilty of kidnapping and attempted murder, but you see the problem with trying to prosecute him, do you not?"

"Yes," Mink replied. "Things that never officially happened would suddenly be part of an official record."

"There you have it," Burns replied. "So what are we to do with him? In your accounting, you tell us how Holdsworth came forward of his own volition to confess his part in the gold business and to confess to abducting Jenkins. This counts for him. And, given the circumstances surrounding his taking of Jenkins, the deaths of the others involved, I, for one, am not sure I would have acted any differently."

"So there is a chance for leniency?" Walker asked.

"You urge that in your report, and we are constrained to agree. More than being merely lenient, we have decided that, given the, uh…" Burns hesitated momentarily and continued, "'complications' involved in his prosecution and the circumstances surrounding his transgressions, we have decided to let Holdsworth get on with his life unhindered if, and only if, these incidents will disappear from his memory and discourse as thoroughly as they have from the official record."

"I am sure he will agree," Walker said. "He in all respects seems to be a reasonable man, and what you offer is more than reasonable."

"Good," Burns said. He set the *Barbadoes* log and report on the table behind his desk. "That is settled, and I believe we are done with old business as it were. Do you have any questions?"

Mink and Walker glanced at each other. Then Walker turned to Burns. "We were wondering what might be next for us, the ship's next assignment."

"Ah, yes, of course," Burns replied. "That was next on my list. I can forsee one or more missions that that you could profitably undertake for us. Nothing right now, but in the not too distant future. For now, it will be blockade duty with the inshore squadron. Hardly exciting stuff, but you know how valuable small frigates are in such duty."

They both knew as well how boring such duty could be, beating back and forth outside a port waiting for ships that never came out.

"And when, sir, are we expected to be on our new station?" Walker asked.

"Why don't you take a few days to rest here in London? You've certainly earned it. Your orders will stipulate that you are due on station once your ship is repaired and refit to your satisfaction. Will that do?"

"Yes sir. That is very generous of you, sir. Thank you."

"My pleasure." Burns got up and refilled all their glasses. "Now that business is out of the way, I must hear about the taking of that Frenchman. Lieutenant, your captain's retelling in his report is far too modest. I must hear it from you, if you would."

Mink smiled and leaned forward. Of course, he would.

Printed in the United States
by Baker & Taylor Publisher Services